PROPERTY

EVELYN FERRAS

PROPERTY

Evelyn Ferras

CHAPTER 1

A smile spreads across my lips when I see my friend running toward me, her dark red hair flying around her like a wild mane.

Many times, I've thought about dyeing my hair like she does. Maybe bright pink or purple. But I know I can't do anything that would attract too much attention to me.

If I want to stay here, at college, I have to remain invisible. Just another girl with straight long dark brown hair and dark brown eyes.

No one here would ever suspect that I'm a mafia princess and the daughter of Paulo Verratti, the boss of a notorious crime family.

My name is Caterina Verratti, but everyone here knows me as Rina Hayes. I like having a fake identity. Sometimes, it feels more genuine than my real one. Here

I can be who I really am and not who my family expects me to be.

"What did you forget now, Ivy?" I ask as my friend reaches me.

Her chest is heaving. "Do you still have that book we need for our project? I need it, and there are no copies left at the library." Her gray eyes stare at me with a pleading look.

"Yeah." I reach into my bag and pull out the book she needs. "I'm done with it anyway."

"Thank you so much! You're a lifesaver!" She grabs the book, a big grin on her face. "I'll return it to you ASAP."

"No problem." I smile back.

"I gotta go. See you later." Ivy waves at me.

"See ya." I head to the dorm.

A strange sensation washes over me, and I glance over my shoulder. I feel like someone's watching me, but I can't see anyone. It's probably just my paranoia.

My father has sent his men to watch over me and keep me safe, but one of his conditions to even let me go to college on my own is that I absolutely can't know the identity of those who are spying on me... err, I mean protecting me.

He doesn't only want to make sure that our family's enemies don't find me but also wants to ensure that I don't do anything stupid. Most of the time, I don't really mind, as long as I have the freedom to do whatever I want, like go to an occasional party and study like a regular college student.

But when I reach my room, I stop dead in my tracks. Something's wrong.

My family doesn't want me to share my room with anyone because they see it as a security risk, so I don't have any roommates who might be able to find out who I really am or try to hurt me.

But now I'm sure someone's touched my door. Before I go to class, I always leave a small piece of duct tape sort of hanging off the door handle.

If someone tries the handle, the tape sticks to it. And now it's firmly stuck to the handle as if someone pressed it.

Maybe it was an accident and someone tried my door by mistake, thinking it's theirs. That stuff happens.

I don't think my family's enemies have found me either, because my family's guards would be here already and my phone wouldn't stop ringing. Just in case, I check my phone, but I don't have any texts or missed calls.

Maybe my father has stopped trusting me and sent someone to search my room. I eye the door for a few long moments and listen.

As carefully as possible, I unlock the door and push it wide open, stepping aside quickly so I can hide behind the wall in case an attacker is waiting for me in my room.

When I take a quick peek inside, I see a familiar face. My shoulders instantly relax. The tall, broad-shouldered guy standing in my room in a suit works for my father.

"Hey, Richard," I say as I enter the room and close the door before someone can see him. I don't want anyone to start any rumors that I'm hooking up with an older guy on campus. "What's up?"

"You need to come with me, miss," he says. "Your father's orders."

I furrow my brow. "Come where? Is something wrong? Am I in danger?"

"No, you're not, but your father requests your immediate presence. Pack anything you want to take with you and come with me."

Which basically means I have to hurry because my father doesn't like to wait.

I go to my closet.

"Can you tell me what's going on? How long will I be gone? I have an exam soon." When my father wants to see me, he'll see me no matter what.

And if I have to miss classes because of it, he'll arrange everything so I don't suffer any consequences for my absence, except I'll have to study harder to catch up.

Maybe I can do some studying on my way to my

father's house. My family lives about two hundred miles away from my campus.

"I don't know," Richard says. "Your father didn't say."

"Why didn't he call?" I glance at Richard. "Wait, don't answer that. Of course he didn't call to give me a heads-up. He wants to see me now, and everyone just has to make it happen."

The last time I was summoned like this, my father only wanted to discuss how I was doing at college, even though he could've easily gotten that information from elsewhere.

But he wanted to talk to me directly, and I had no choice but to comply. Pissing off my father can mean the end of my college life, so I'll do my best to avoid doing it.

I definitely won't tell him that I think that dragging me out of college like this just to chat is ridiculous and a waste of everyone's time.

Once I pack my bag, I turn to Richard. "I'm ready."

"Back exit. Wait two minutes." He slips out of the room with my bag, and I wait as instructed.

He and I aren't supposed to be seen together. After glancing at the clock, I get out in the hallway and hurry to the back exit. If Ivy or any of my other friends ask, I'll have to lie to them that there was a family emergency.

I stride through the parking lot until I see Richard's

car. After looking right and left and making sure no one's watching me, I get in the car.

As soon as we reach the main street, three more cars join us. It's standard protocol, and the guards are here to keep me safe.

I stare through the window, trying to ignore the nervous feeling in my stomach.

I haven't done anything wrong or broken my father's rules, so there's no reason for concern, but he's a scary man, especially because one word from him can change my life forever.

I try hard not to think about it.

RICHARD OPENS THE DOOR FOR ME AND I GET OUT OF THE car. I stare at the three-story mansion in front of me.

My home.

But honestly, I feel more like home in my dorm. This place might be like a cross between an expensive hotel and a museum, with a pool, a movie theater, gym, and a lot of other fun things that people dream about, but there are also way too many guards, cameras, and eyes everywhere.

All the security in the world won't make me feel safe here. There's a constant worry at the back of my mind that I'll do or say something to anger my father, and that's never fun.

One time, I touched a book in his private library that he didn't want me to touch and he lost his mind and locked me up in my room for days.

So yeah, I might have everything I want at my fingertips here, but if I reach out for the wrong thing at the wrong moment, or if I'm too loud when my father can hear me, or if my mere presence annoys him, I'll be in trouble.

Richard escorts me straight to my father's office. I take a deep breath before entering.

My father sits in his big leather chair. His dark eyes are focused on a sheet of paper on the desk in front of him, and his grayish dark brown hair is slightly disheveled.

I lick my lips as Richard leaves. "Father," I say, doing my best to keep my voice calm and steady.

If my father senses just a bit of my discomfort or unease, he's going to call me out for it and try to make it worse.

"Ah, Caterina. You're finally here." He looks up at me, his eyes scanning me up and down. "Sit."

I settle in the chair across from him, keeping my shoulders straight, just as he likes it. I've heard him berate my mother more than once for slumping because he thinks it's unladylike and not giving him the respect he deserves as the head of the family.

He lowers his gaze back to the papers on his desk, and a few long minutes pass as I sit there in silence.

I really hate when he does this. He's made it sound like he's been waiting for me for ages and now he's ignoring me, as if I don't matter at all.

"You're to be married to Dante Antonelli at the end of the week," he says. "Your mother will help you with the preparations."

My jaw hits the floor, my chest constricting. I can't breathe as I stare at him, wondering if I've heard him right.

"I don't understand," I blurt out, even though I know saying it is a mistake.

My father looks at me as if I'm the stupidest person he's ever met. "Which part of what I just said wasn't clear enough?"

I don't want to get married, especially not to someone I don't even know. "But what about college and--?"

"I entertained your fantasy for a while to make you happy, but now it's time for you to fulfill your duty to this family. The Antonellis and I made a deal years ago, and their boss has agreed the time has come."

"The Antonellis?" I choke out.

My mind is in overdrive, and I can't even remember the basic info about the family in question.

All I can recall is that they're ruthless and dangerous. They leave bloodshed wherever they go and are even worse than my father.

Even if I'm wrong about them or if I'm thinking about the wrong family, I don't want to be forced to marry their boss or whoever.

"Father, please," I say, tears filling the corners of my eyes. "I'm not ready. I want to finish college first, and I—"

"Caterina, don't be ridiculous," he cuts me off, his eyes narrowing. "You have everything you need to be a dutiful wife. You are more than ready. There's no need for you to finish college. Your husband will provide for you as I provide for your mother. You'll see soon that this is the best thing that could've happened to you. The Antonellis are powerful and strong. They'll keep you safe."

Safe? The same way he's protecting my mother by keeping her locked up in our house for most of the time?

She isn't even allowed to go anywhere on her own, not even with the guards because it's supposedly not safe, but I know that's a pile of bullshit.

I open my mouth, but words don't come out because I can see in my father's eyes that there's nothing I can say to change his mind. He's made his decision, and this is normal to him.

If I point out arranged marriages are ridiculous in

this day and age, he'll call me hysterical and have me taken to my room, probably with some sedatives included.

I've been through all that already, before I learned how to tiptoe around my father and only say the things he wants to hear.

But now I don't know what to do. My throat is tight and my chest hurts. My whole world has just twisted and collapsed.

I thought my father wouldn't need me, and that he'd see reason and let me live my own life, but I was wrong.

He played me.

He let me believe I was getting what I wanted.

My eyes are blurry from tears, so I don't see when my father pushes the button on his desk, but a moment later, the guards enter the room, which means he has summoned them.

"We're done here," my father announces.

I get to my feet like a robot, and the guards escort me to my room.

To my prison.

All I want to do is escape, but it's impossible.

My life is over.

CHAPTER 2

I pace up and down my room, but I can't come up with a solution to my problem. The guards are outside my door all the time, and they won't let me out at all.

I've tried pleading with them more than once and even asked them to just let me go to our private library on the other end of the house so I can find a book to pass the time, but they refused.

They're loyal to my father to the core, and they're not going to disobey him no matter what. They'd die for him.

I don't even have a TV, a laptop, or a phone. Everything has been taken away from me with the excuse that I need peace and quiet to focus on my wedding.

No one cares about me.

I'm just a pawn.

A piece of property.

They don't see me as a person at all. I have no friends here. No help. My room is too high up, so I can't climb out of the window without risking breaking my neck.

Maybe death would be preferable to marrying some scary guy I don't know, but I don't want to think about it. I can't accept that this is it for me and that I can't do anything to get myself out of this mess.

When the door opens, my mother enters, a white dress in her hands. There are dark circles under her brown eyes, and her long dark brown hair is falling freely around her shoulders, just like my father loves it.

"Mom! Please help me!" I run to her as soon as the door closes and we're alone, my hands clasped in front of me. "I don't want to marry!"

"Hush," she says, giving me a stern glare. "You shouldn't say such things. Look what I've brought you."

She spreads out the white lace dress, but I can barely pay attention to it because I don't care about the stupid wedding dress for a wedding I absolutely don't want.

"Isn't it beautiful?" she asks and lays the dress on my bed. "You'll look wonderful in it."

"Mom." I catch her arm and she flinches, her eyes flitting to me, so I let her go.

It's my father's fault she acts like that.

"Please. Help me get out of here," I say. "Don't you know who the Antonellis are? I'm pretty sure I heard their boss killed his own father and brother. His own blood! What do you think he'll do to me?"

"Nonsense, honey. I understand you're nervous and afraid, but everything's going to be okay. I was nervous on the day of my wedding too."

"And are you happy now? Are you truly happy?" I look deep into her eyes, but all I see is emptiness.

"Yes, of course I am."

"That's bullshit!"

"Language, Caterina." She shakes her head. "Obey your husband, and you won't have anything to worry about."

"Obey?" I let out a nervous laugh. "And then what? I have to give up my dreams and drop out of college so I can be trapped in some fancy house."

"Don't be so selfish. It's not about you. It's about our family. Marrying Antonelli is a great honor, and you can't even comprehend how important this is for our family. You may think that you know what you want right now, but once you have children, you'll see that family is what matters most. It's our strength."

"If family is what matters most, then help me. I'm your daughter. Why can't I just marry someone I like? Why does it have to be a stranger? Can't I honor my family by marrying someone else?" I'm all out of ideas on how to get my mother on my side.

Deep down, I think she really believes she's doing a

great thing by being married to my father, despite how he treats her. I guess that's how she copes.

Will I become like her? A shell of myself? But I don't know what she was like before she married my father.

She's never talked about her life. It's like she didn't even exist before she married him, which sounds crazy to me.

"Trust your father. He knows what he's doing. He wouldn't have agreed to give your hand in marriage if he didn't believe Antonelli is a good match, even if the deal was made years ago."

Oh, my father would've absolutely agreed to hand me over to the devil himself if he thought it would benefit him.

"With time, you'll get to know your husband and you'll learn how to love him," my mom says.

"Why? Why do I have to do it? Why can't Father just strike a deal without forcing me to marry? Why don't my feelings and my opinion matter at all? Why does he get to decide? Tell me, Mom. Tell me why. How does any of this make sense?"

"We have to honor our tradition. It's what keeps us strong and united." She reaches out for me, but I step back. "We can't forget who and what we are."

"Well, that's just fucking great." I glare at her, crossing my arms. "My life means nothing."

"You're wrong. It means everything. I don't think you

realize how important women are in our family. Without us and our support, there'd be no family."

"But you don't get a say in anything your husband does! You're not equals."

She looks at me as if I've just said the strangest thing ever. "Your father is the boss, so of course everyone must obey him. I'm free to voice my opinions to him, but he makes the final decision, and I assure you, he thinks about all of us when he does that. I don't know what's happened to you. We never should've let you go to college. Someone there has filled your head with nonsense."

We? Does she really think anything she might have said was more than background noise for my father?

I don't think I've ever seen her voice her opinions, unless it was to agree with my father or say something she believed he would approve of. Maybe she doesn't even realize it, but I've been watching my parents interact for years.

I was supposed to be like a piece of furniture back then too. To be seen and not heard.

"Put on the dress. I'll return in a few minutes." My mom smiles at me and heads to the door.

I glance at the dress and want to scream. But if I tear it to shreds, they'll just get me another one.

I rake my hand through my hair.

I don't know what to do.

I push back the tears filling my eyes when my mother lowers the veil over my face. Then I'm escorted out of my room with so many guards around me as if I'm the most dangerous person in the house full of assassins and mercenaries.

But I guess I am.

If the wedding falls through, it will be a huge blow for my father and our family. And if the Antonellis took offense, there'd be a war.

I wish I could do something and ruin everything. If I'm going down, then I might as well bring everyone with me.

But there's nothing I can do. If I yell, they're going to find a way to shut me up and laugh at me.

My words don't matter. I'm not physically strong enough to fight them either.

I can only hope that I'll somehow get lucky and find a way to escape. Maybe if I go along with this farce and pretend I've accepted my fate, everyone would lower their guard around me.

My pulse speeds up when I enter the room.

I don't know if it was my father who insisted for the wedding ceremony to be held in our living room, which has been cleaned out for the occasion and new furniture has been brought, or if it was my future husband.

I don't even want to think about him.

The veil makes it harder to see things clearly around me, but the first person I spot is my father.

He's grinning like this is the best day of his life, and when he glances at me, the corners of his lips tighten for a split second.

If I mess this up right now, he's going to kill me himself. There's no doubt about that. I can see it in his eyes.

I look at all the other men in the room. Which one is going to be my husband?

They're all my father's age. Some even older. My mother tugs on my arm and guides me to the spot where I'm supposed to stand.

My father lowers his gaze to his watch.

He's not here.

My future husband isn't here yet.

My stomach flutters. Maybe there's still hope. Maybe he's changed his mind and doesn't want to marry me either.

I don't know if that would be good for me. My father would be furious and he'd blame me for it. But I hope for it anyway.

I don't know how long we wait, but then the hottest man I've ever seen enters the room. My father instantly cheers up, and I assume the man is one of the Antonellis.

"Dante," my father greets him. "Welcome!"

Dante's handsome face remains expressionless. I don't think he's the boss.

He's too young, maybe a little older than me. His short black hair is slightly messy, and his blue eyes are as cold as ice.

His full lips are pressed into a straight line, and it doesn't look like he's impressed by whatever my father is saying to him.

I can't help but admire how his black suit fits his strong, lean body—it must've been tailored for him.

I'm too busy staring at his chiseled jaw to notice anything else.

"Let's get this over with," Dante says in a bored tone.

Two of my father's men immediately jump forward. One of them opens a black suitcase and sets it on the table in front of Dante.

Wait, I'm marrying *him*?

For some reason, that hurts me even more. He can't be that much older than me, and with that face and body, he can have any woman he wants, even if he didn't have all the power that comes with being a mafia boss.

But if he's here and willing to go through with this, then I'm sure he doesn't share my views on arranged marriages and the world. He's not going to help me.

Actually, he hasn't even glanced at me.

It's like I don't exist.

After he and my father sign some papers, one of my

father's men approaches me. The guy gives me a pen and points at the empty line on the sheet of paper he's holding.

This is it.

Once I sign, I'll become Dante's property. But I have no choice. I can already feel my father's glare on me because I'm taking too long.

My throat constricts and my hand shakes, but I sign the damn thing.

"There. All done," Dante says, and snaps his fingers.

His men surround him.

"Take my wife," he says, and the men start toward me.

It takes all my willpower not to back away from them.

"Are you not going to--?" my father says.

"I have other business to attend to," Dante says.

"Ah, yes. Of course." My father inclines his head. "I'm looking forward to our partnership. Together, we're going to be unstoppable."

Dante only nods his head and strides out of the room. His men grab me by the arms and pull me with them.

I manage to glance over my shoulder at my mother. She gives me a smile of approval, and I hate that I still have the damn veil on so she can't see just how angry and disappointed I am that she let this happen to me.

I'm mad at the whole world, but mostly at her because I thought of all people she'd understand.

But she doesn't.

No one does.

Dante doesn't even look back as he exits the house. He just gets in his car and speeds off.

His men drag me to one of the other cars and shove me inside, trapping me in the back seat between them.

Dante really doesn't care who he married. It was all just a business transaction to him. And it's not like he can't have any lovers.

Maybe there's someone else in his life.

But then I remember the look in his eyes, and I don't think that's true. That man cares for no one. If I ask him to let me go, I don't think he'll do it, even if he doesn't want me.

I stare at my hands on my lap. There may not be a ring on my finger, but I feel like there's a collar around my neck now. It's like a heaviness I can't get rid of, and I don't know if I'll ever be able to do it.

CHAPTER 3

Everything around me is a blur as I'm taken to a huge mansion that seems to be in the middle of nowhere.

I can't see any other houses close by, and I'm pretty sure we've been driving through endless trees for at least an hour.

They don't care if I see where I'm going. It's not like anyone expects me to escape. As the men lead me through a long hallway, I try to memorize as much of it as possible so I can find my way out of the house.

Maybe it's crazy to think I'll get a chance to run away, but maybe no one will expect me to try. If I can get out of the house and into the woods, I may be able to disappear before anyone can find me.

I hold onto that hope as I'm shoved into a spacious room. The door clicks as I'm locked inside.

I rush to the windows, despite knowing that I'm on

the third floor, but as I spread the curtains, my throat constricts.

Bars. There are bars on the windows. Climbing down is impossible. Throwing myself to my death is impossible too.

Fuck!

I look around the room. A king-sized bed is in the middle, and a big, heavy closet across from it. There's nothing else except for a nightstand.

A door catches my attention, and I cross the room to get to it. I expect it to be locked, but it's not.

I find myself staring at a small bathroom. Of course, I'm like a prisoner. I won't even be allowed out into the hallway.

A nervous laugh escapes me. There's a simple shower, a toilet, and a sink. No mirror. A toothbrush is peeking out from the plastic cup on the sink.

I grab it to inspect it closer. But it's a cheap piece of plastic that won't be of any use as a weapon.

Unless I want to get myself sick by eating the toothpaste, I don't know what else I can do.

I get out of the bathroom and head to the closet. When I open it, I realize there's only a dozen plain black cocktail dresses, or maybe they're nightgowns. And an identical number of plain black flat shoes. I spot a box at the bottom. It's full of black panties and bras.

My husband is obviously insane or he doesn't care. I

scowl, but I need to get out of my stupid wedding dress because I can't stand the feel of it against my skin anymore.

After I grab one of the black dresses, I change in the bathroom.

As I stare at my wedding dress on the floor, I can't help but wonder if I could use it to choke someone with it, but I conclude it's just not going to work.

I chew on the inside of my cheek as I take a seat on the bed, which is surprisingly comfortable.

Now what? I'm trapped, and I don't know how to get out of here. Even worse, I have no idea what my husband is going to do to me.

Husband.

The word makes me nauseated.

Dante isn't my husband.

He's my warden.

My jailer.

I stare at my hands on my lap. If only I was strong enough to strangle him, but I know I'm not.

A sound coming from the hallway makes me look up at the door. Someone's coming. My heart leaps into my throat as I get to my feet, eyeing the door carefully.

The lock clicks, and I hold my breath as the door opens.

A woman with dark hair tied in a bun enters the room with a tray in her hands. She's wearing a black dress that falls just past her knees, and I catch a glimpse of another person standing out in the hallway, but I can't tell who they are.

"Mrs. Antonelli," she says as she bows her head, and the door closes behind her.

It takes me a moment to figure out she's talking to me.

I watch her as she places the tray with food on the nightstand.

"Please help me!" I run to her, letting my desperation show in my voice. "Please! I don't want to be here!"

She turns to me, her dark eyes wide. "I'm sorry, ma'am. I can't do what you ask. Enjoy your meal."

"No, wait!" I catch her arm before she can leave. "I can't stay here! He's going to kill me! You have to help me. No one has to know! You can just sneak in a phone for me so I can call my family! Please!"

Words just spill out of my mouth, and I don't know if I'm even making any sense, but I don't know what to say to get her on my side.

"I have to go," she says, prying my fingers off her arm. "You're safe here, ma'am."

"No, you don't understand. I'm not safe!"

She slips outside, and the other person who's out there with her quickly closes and locks the door. I run my hand through my hair. Shit!

I should've said something else. I should've asked for

something else. I'm an idiot. I let my panic overtake my brain and now I blew my chance at getting out of this room.

I guess some part of me believed the woman would sympathize with me and understand what's going on here. It's painfully obvious I'm not here willingly. I'm locked in a goddamn room with bars on the windows.

Fuck! I kick my leg out at the empty air.

But what's done is done. I can't go back and convince the woman that I'm super happy to be here and that I absolutely wouldn't try to escape if she just let me out into the hallway to take a walk.

The smell of food makes my stomach rumble. I haven't eaten anything for hours, and the food looks delicious, so I go closer.

Maybe it's been poisoned and I'm going to die. Or there's a drug in it so I'd do exactly what my husband wants me.

Even though I want to devour the food, I know I can't. I need to keep my head clear. A fork catches my eye and I pick it up.

It's not too sharp, but it's not plastic either. Silver, probably. I grip it tightly as I stare at it. An idea comes to my mind. Too bad there's no knife, but this will have to do.

I hide the fork behind my back after I sit down on the bed, and I wait.

It seems like an eternity, but when the door finally clicks, I brace myself.

The woman who brought me the food is back, and there's another woman in the hallway who's probably tasked with watching the door to make sure I don't escape.

The first woman enters, briefly dipping her head. Her brow creases when she sees the tray with food still intact.

"Was the meal not to your liking, ma'am?" she asks. "Do you want me to bring you something else?"

"I'm not hungry," I lie, watching her every move.

"All right, ma'am." She reaches for the tray, and I spring to my feet.

Before she can react, I wind my arm around her from behind and lift the fork to her face.

"Let go of me, ma'am!" she cries.

"No! Don't move!" I yell, bringing the fork close to her eye. "Do as I say and you'll get to keep your eye, okay? Now go to the door. Slowly!"

I keep my grip on her tight as we inch to the door.

She's trembling, but she's not trying to push me away, probably because she's shocked and terrified, and worried that my hand might slip.

"Open the door." I'm not sure what I'm going to do once I'm out, but I need to find a way to get out of this damn house.

"Ma'am—"

"Quiet!" I snap.

Her hand shakes as she reaches for the door handle. When she opens the door, the woman in the hallway gasps and takes a step back.

I barely make it out of the door when I hear a shout. Shit!

I turn my head in the direction of the noise. A group of five or six guards is running toward us, and on the other side, there are only walls, which I somehow managed to forget or failed to see when they brought me here.

I have nowhere to run.

My grip on the woman falters, my heart pounding in my chest. She slips out of my grasp a moment before hands grab me.

One of the guards yanks my hand back, making me yelp as he squeezes so hard that I drop the fork.

"What the fuck is going on here?" a voice booms through the hallway, and everyone instantly goes quiet.

I know that voice.

It belongs to Dante.

Fuck!

"Sir, your wife threatened me with a fork," the woman says, a bewildered look on her face. "She wanted to get out of the room. She said she would gouge my eye out!"

"My..." Dante's voice trails off as the guards part for him and his gaze falls on me.

His eyebrows lift in surprise as his eyes travel up and down my body. A man with dark hair and dark brown eyes stops right next to him.

"Matteo, I had no idea she was so fucking hot," Dante says to the man.

Matteo laughs.

"Are you all right, Elena?" Dante asks the woman I attacked.

"Yes, sir," she says.

"You may go."

She and the other woman bow their heads and hurry down the hallway.

Dante stalks toward me, his eyes icy cold. I can't back away because two men are holding me by the arms.

"What do you think you're doing?" His hand shoots out and tightly grasps my chin.

I just glare at him. Is it such a surprise to him that I'm ready to do just about anything to escape him?

"I guess it's my fault for not explaining the rules to you first." A smile stretches across his lips, but it doesn't reach his eyes. "You'll do exactly what I tell you to, and you'll stay in your room until I say so. Do you understand? You belong to me now, princess."

I grit my teeth.

"I asked you a question." Dante's smile fades as he flicks his fingers.

The guards holding me let go and step aside.

Dante shoves me back until I collide with the wall. My breath leaves my chest in a whoosh. His body presses against mine, and his finger trails over my chin and down my neck.

His hand wraps around my throat next, and my eyes widen as he squeezes.

"If you keep disobeying me, maybe I'll just snap your neck," he whispers, his face only a breath away from mine, his grip on my neck still tight, making me fight for air.

His eyes focus on my mouth, and he leans closer as if he's going to kiss me.

The only thing I can do is try to nod.

"Is that a yes?" A chilling smile crosses his lips again.

I bob my head as his hold on my neck loosens a little.

"You're lucky I don't want you dead right now," he says. "But next time, I want a proper answer."

He lets go of me and walks away.

I gasp, my hand flying to my neck as I sink to the floor. Adrenaline still courses through my body as the guards lift me up and push me back into my room, locking the door.

I stumble forward and barely manage to reach the

bed before collapsing. My throat throbs and I can feel Dante's fingers on my skin as if they're still there.

Tears sting the corners of my eyes.

How the hell am I going to get myself out of here alive?

CHAPTER 4

I stare at the ceiling as I lie on the bed. My mind is racing with all kinds of thoughts, but my biggest worry is my escape.

After my failed attempt, I have no idea how I'm going to get out of this prison. The guards are everywhere, and even though I can't hear them, they're probably outside every step of the way.

And Dante...

Dante scares me.

Whenever I think about him, I can feel the ghost of his fingers on my neck. It's not hard to believe that he'd really snap my neck if he wanted to, and he wouldn't even think about it for more than a second.

Maybe he'll end up killing me, and it might be my only way out of this life. Because living like this isn't a life at all.

I don't know if my husband even realizes that I'm a human being, and not a robot who just switches on when he needs it and stays switched off the rest of the time.

What does he expect me to do all day? If I stay alone with my thoughts all the time, I'm going to lose my mind.

I still don't have a clue what he intends to do with me either. Maybe he'll forget that I exist or ignore me, which may be a blessing but also a curse.

I don't think I can talk anyone into letting me go or helping me, and after my encounter with Dante, there's no chance he's just going to agree to let me go live somewhere on my own.

Actually, he probably won't even think about me and what I might need. He'll only think about what he needs and wants from me.

And once he tires of me or decides he no longer wants me, he'll just kill me.

I curl my fingers into fists.

It's my fault I trusted my father. I never should've let him trick me into this. Before, I believed obeying him and doing as best as I could to please him would give me what I wanted, but now I see that I was deluding myself.

I should've run away when I had the chance. My father's men might've been watching me at college, but I could've found a way to slip away and disappear.

My family would've searched everywhere for me, but

I could've changed my appearance and gotten a fake identity.

Even if they found me and killed me, it would've been better to live free for a while than like this.

I thought that going to college would make my father realize that I could be of so much more use to him than just as a bargaining chip.

I should've known better, especially after what happened with my older half-sister.

There were plenty of chances for me to escape even before I went to college. Maybe I was sheltered and constantly watched, but whenever I was allowed to go outside, I could've slipped away.

I could've probably found a way out of my father's house. His guards' schedules were easy to find back then, and I could've planned my escape.

Instead, I was a fool who dreamed about getting a degree and working with my father one day.

I let out a growl of frustration.

Stupid!

So fucking stupid!

My father only ever had one use for me, and I refused to see it. I refused to see that he never cared about me. He might've kept me safe from his enemies, but he did it in the same way he took care of his property.

I close my eyes and sigh.

Thinking about what I could've or should've done is

completely pointless. I can't go back and change anything. Instead of begging my father to let me go to college, I should've plotted my way to freedom.

And even when I got here, I didn't think things through and planned what to do carefully enough.

I guess it's just hard to accept this is really happening. A part of me keeps hoping this is a realistic nightmare, and I'll wake up in my bed in my dorm room.

But I know it's not.

It's real.

Too real.

But maybe it's not over yet. I'm not dead yet, and as long as I breathe, there's hope. Maybe being trapped in this room is a test, and I'm failing it.

If I find a way to convince everyone that I'll be on my best behavior and that I'm willing to be Dante's wife, then maybe I'll get what I want eventually.

But I have to be patient and careful, even if I don't know how I'll have the strength to survive all this.

I just can't accept that this is my fate.

I can't.

There will be an opportunity.

There has to be.

And when it happens, I'll jump at it.

Even if it kills me.

CHAPTER 5

Every time I hear footsteps out in the hallway, my pulse speeds up. I keep waiting for Dante to show up and take what he believes is his or kill me.

It's dark outside and moonlight is shining through the windows. The shadow of the bars on the walls makes me feel even more like I'm in prison, but I don't want to be in complete darkness either.

This is my punishment.

It has to be.

I must've done something to have all this happen to me, but I don't know what it is.

When I hear voices in the hallway, I sit up, straining my ears so I can hear something. But they're too far away.

I wait for a few moments, but when I realize they

aren't coming any closer, I get to my feet and tiptoe to the door.

The voices are louder and clearer now, and I press my ear against the door. I don't know if I care because I'm bored out of my mind, or if I'm hoping I'll hear something that will somehow help me.

I recognize the voices, and my heart skips a beat.

Dante.

And that other guy.

Matteo, I think.

"I have everyone looking for it, but I was told the DEA has it," Matteo says.

"How the fuck did that happen?" Dante's voice is full of anger.

"I don't know, but it looks like someone tipped them off about the shipment."

"Who?"

I think Matteo hesitates, because I can't hear anything for a few moments.

"Tell me," Dante barks with impatience.

"Your uncle."

I didn't know Dante had an uncle. That's at least one of his family members who's still alive, but obviously that information won't be of any use to me.

"How the fuck did he know? Who told him?" Dante asks, and his voice drips with ice.

"I don't know."

"Reach out to our contact at the DEA office. Find out what they know. I want everything."

"Yes, sir."

"Locate my uncle. He's playing with fire, and I won't allow him to mess with my business or set foot in my territory. If he has a problem with me, he can request an audience, come here, and tell me all about it himself."

"It won't be easy to find him," Matteo says. "He doesn't want to be found."

"Then what the fuck does he want? One shipment won't change anything. We'll replace it and change our route. If there's a rat, we'll find it and kill it."

"It looks like he's not happy about your deal with the Verrattis and your marriage to Caterina Verratti."

Dante snorts. "I don't give a fuck. What I do is none of his business."

Why would his uncle have a problem with him marrying me?

Oh wait. Was it because his uncle wanted to marry me himself?

My father made a deal with a Verratti, so maybe it didn't matter which one I ended up marrying.

But I don't think Dante's uncle is as powerful or can offer the same thing that Dante can, so my father would've never agreed to give me to him even if he'd asked.

A phone rings, making me flinch.

Matteo says something, but I can't make out the words. He's probably walked away farther down the hallway.

I wait a little longer.

"There's news," Matteo says. "Our scouts followed one of the guys who works for your uncle. He just went into a house that was bought through one of your uncle's offshore companies. What do you want me to tell them? We can attack and capture your uncle if he's there, or capture and question anyone we find in the house."

"No. Tell them to back off and wait. Observe only. Don't engage."

"But—" Matteo pauses. "Yes, sir. I'll tell them."

He must've realized questioning his boss' orders would be a very dumb move.

"It's probably a trap. My uncle isn't that careless. He wants me to be pissed off and jump at the first chance I get to retaliate. But it's not going to work. He can play his games all he wants, but I'm going to win every single one of them."

The confidence in Dante's voice is astounding. I've never heard anyone talk like that, not even my father.

Dante is so damn sure of himself and everything he says. I don't think I want to find out what happens when he doesn't get what he wants—if that ever happens.

Maybe I should just ask him what he expects from

me. He might actually tell me. But do I really want to know?

Sometimes, ignorance is better.

"All right, sir. I'll keep you updated," Matteo says.

"You may go. All of you."

Is he talking to the guards too? I haven't heard anyone else speak, but that doesn't mean they're not there. They have to be, especially after what I tried.

But why does he want them to leave now?

A few moments later, I hear footsteps getting closer and closer. I back away from the door. My heart pounds in my chest when they stop in front of the door.

He's coming.

I look around for something I can use to defend myself, even though I know there isn't anything, but panic grips my insides again, and I don't know what I'm going to do.

The door clicks and I step back until my legs collide with the bed.

What does he want?

Why is he here now?

The answer floats in my brain, but I refuse to acknowledge it.

The door opens, and I let out a shuddery breath.

CHAPTER 6

DANTE STEPS THROUGH THE DOOR, AND THE LOOK OF ICY fury on his face under the moonlight makes me gasp.

He's clearly angrier than he sounded while talking to Matteo, and I'm not sure what to do. Asking him anything or talking to him now seems like a terrible idea.

"Hello, wife," he says, a smile curving his lips, but it's so cold and contorted that it's almost a grimace.

My gaze falls on the door.

He didn't lock it, and if he told the guards to leave, then they're not in the hallway.

I don't think. I just bolt past him to the door.

But as my fingers grasp the door handle, Dante's arms tightly wrap around my waist.

"Where the fuck do you think you're going?" he hisses, yanking me away from the door.

I manage to rip myself out of his arms and almost fall to the floor. "Away from you!"

He laughs. "You can't get away from me, Caterina. You're mine."

While he pulls the key to lock the door out of his pocket, I spot a gun tucked in the holster under his black suit jacket.

My mind goes into overdrive, and all I can hear is my heartbeat reverberating through me as I launch at him.

But I'm too slow.

As if he can sense what I'm about to do, he spins around and whips the gun out, pointing it at me.

My breath gets caught in my chest and I freeze on the spot.

"Do you have a death wish?" Dante asks, aiming straight at my head.

As I stare down the barrel of his gun, I realize one thing.

I don't want to die.

It's the only thought that flashes through my mind. Everything else is just blank and doesn't matter anymore.

All I want is to stay alive.

I try to back away, but he catches my arm, roughly pulling me to him. A yelp escapes my throat as his fingers painfully tangle in my hair.

He presses the gun to my lips.

"Open your mouth," he commands. "Open it!"

My lips part on their own, and he shoves the barrel into my mouth. Tears fill the corners of my eyes, and I can't think anymore.

My eyes lift to his, pleading with him to let me go.

"Do you want to die, huh?" he asks.

I close my eyes for a moment as tears now stream freely down my face. Even if I want to say something, I can't.

If he pulls the trigger, it's all over.

His gaze is fully trained on my mouth.

"You know what I'd like more than this? Your pretty little mouth around my cock," he says, tilting my head back. "But what would you like? My cock or a bullet?"

I can only let out a sound from the back of my throat.

"What did you say? My cock?"

I manage a small nod.

Survive.

Survive.

Survive.

It's the only thing I want.

"Good choice," he says, pulling the gun out of my mouth. "Get down on your knees."

He lets go of me, and I fall to my knees, gasping for breath.

A shudder runs through my body, and when I glance

up, I see Dante unzipping his pants with one hand while still gripping the gun in the other.

My eyes lift to his.

There's something dark in them.

Primal.

Wild.

A different kind of shudder shoots through me.

My gaze drops to his thick length, and my eyes widen. I didn't think he'd be so big, or maybe I just don't have enough experience with men to know, but he still looks huge.

"If you bite me, I'm going to shoot you. Got it?" He keeps the gun trained on me. "Put your hands behind your back."

I slowly move my hands behind me.

Dante's hand winds in my hair.

"Open," he says.

I stare into his eyes for a few moments before parting my lips.

"Wider."

He guides my head to his cock. When he slips past my lips, he sighs.

I'm not sure what I'm supposed to do because I've never done this before. And how could I?

I've never had a boyfriend and I've never hooked up with anyone because I didn't want to risk upsetting my father. If I'd done something like that and he found out, he would've killed me.

Dante pushes his hips forward, slamming his cock against the back of my throat and making me gag.

He pulls out a little and dives back in, and for a few moments, I struggle to breathe.

His grip on my hair tightens as he pushes in and out of my mouth, sliding against my tongue.

I steal a glance at his face.

He doesn't look angry anymore. There's something else on his face now.

Pleasure?

A tingle starts low in my stomach, and I don't even know why.

I'm not afraid anymore.

I just let him use my mouth, doing my best not to choke or forget how to breathe.

"Look at me," he says, slowing down his movements, his grip on my hair loosening.

I lift my gaze to his.

He smiles at me and groans, and then I feel him come into my mouth.

After he pulls out, he presses his thumb over my lips. "Swallow."

He watches me as I do as he asks and traces his finger over my lips.

"Good girl," he says.

As I try to process what just happened and figure out the weird feeling between my legs, he zips his pants and tucks his gun back into his holster.

When I push myself to my feet, his arms wind around me, his strong body pressed against mine.

His hand lands on my thigh, lifting my dress up. Before I can even think about what he's doing, his fingers run over my wet panties.

A fire lights up inside me at his touch, and, even though I try, I don't feel ashamed about it. He yanks down my panties, and instead of protests, a soft moan slips out of my throat.

I hear him chuckle as his fingers rub my opening.

"You like this," he whispers into my ear as his fingers part my folds, and I'm too focused on the sensations his touch leaves to say anything.

It's strange and fascinating at the same time.

I've never been touched by someone like this, and I want more.

His finger briefly dips inside me, teasing me. He holds me tightly to him as his finger finds my clit. I shudder, the tingling inside me intensifying.

I can't think about anything as my hips push against his finger all on their own. His finger circles my clit, presses, and probes.

The pressure inside me gets stronger, and if he weren't holding me, my knees would've probably given out by now.

It's like he knows exactly how and where to touch me.

Which buttons to push.

He rubs my pussy harder.

Faster.

Rougher.

My breath comes out in small gasps, and just as I'm getting closer to my release, his hand pulls away.

"You shouldn't have tried to run away." His voice is like a caress, his lips brushing my ear. "You don't deserve a reward."

He smacks his palm against my ass and lets go of me.

I stare at him, bewildered, as he leaves. My feet are rooted to the spot when I hear the door lock.

My insides still tingle, my panties down my legs, my dress up.

What the hell just happened?

He can't just leave me like this.

Wanting.

Needing.

Except, he's done it.

I stumble to the bed and sit on the edge, spreading my legs.

I close my eyes, letting my hand slip between my legs. It's not the same feeling, or even close to it, but I need some relief.

Dante's face flashes in my mind as he smiles at me and finishes in my mouth. My orgasm rolls through me, and I let out a soft cry.

When I open my eyes, I stare at my hand in horror. The realization of everything that happened hits me, and all the pleasure I've felt instantly vanishes.

What the fuck is wrong with me?

Disgust and shame claw their way into my mind, and I'm absolutely mortified at what I let Dante do to me.

I should've just picked the bullet.

Now I don't know how I'm going to get what happened out of my mind, and I'm sure Dante will try to use it against me somehow.

He always gets what he wants, doesn't he?

And instead of fighting him, I let him shatter me.

CHAPTER 7

I'm a coward.

It's the only explanation I have. I should've let him kill me.

No matter how many times I showered and brushed my teeth, I still feel like Dante's scent is all over me.

And I can't even tell what his scent reminds me of because it's so different.

So unique.

So intoxicating.

Gah! Why am I even thinking about him?

I need to focus on what matters. So what if I temporarily lost my common sense and completely embarrassed myself?

It doesn't matter. I'm alive, and I should find a way to escape my ridiculously good-looking, psychotic husband.

My stomach rumbles. I haven't eaten anything for a while, mostly because I've been too stressed out and unsure about the food, so I drink some more water instead.

My stomach protests again, but I ignore it.

The adrenaline has worn off, and I'm exhausted, so I lie down on the bed. Dying of starvation sounds absolutely terrible, but maybe Dante will see what I'm doing and agree to one of my requests. I need to find a way to use this, even if my mind feels sluggish right now.

When Elena comes to pick up the tray, her brow furrows.

The guards are at the door too, probably to make sure I don't try anything with her again. I haven't been given a fork again, just a plastic spoon.

And I definitely no longer have much strength left for such an ordeal.

She lifts her worried gaze at me, and I roll to my side, turning my back to her. I hear her leave, and my eyes close.

The sound of the door opening rouses me from my nap, and when I turn to check who it is, I see Dante.

A shiver runs through me, but I don't want to think what it means. I'm not attracted to that monster.

I can't be.

He seems in a much better mood today, or at least

there's no anger in his eyes or tightness around his mouth.

Elena enters after him with a new tray while Dante watches me, his intent gaze slightly unnerving.

His eyes are still as cold as ever, but there's something else in them, and I think it might be lust.

Elena sets the tray on the nightstand and leaves.

"Eat," Dante says when we're alone.

He's not wearing a suit now. Instead, he's in dark gray jeans and a black T-shirt, and I can't help but think that he probably looks good in anything he puts on.

Not that any of it matters or will help me escape, but I'm not blind either.

I settle against the pillows, crossing my arms and glaring at him.

"I won't say it again." His gaze is hard on mine.

I don't move.

He starts toward me and climbs on the bed so fast I don't have the time to react. He gets on top of me, trapping me under his warm body.

I'm momentarily distracted by his proximity, and I don't even notice what he pulls out of the back pocket on his jeans until something cold touches my wrist.

My pulse quickens, and I try to push him away, but I don't have the energy to stop him from cuffing my wrist to the headboard of the bed.

He traces his finger down my bare arm as if he finds something fascinating about it, making me shiver.

When he gets off me, I tug at the cuff, but there's no way I can get free, not even with the help of my other hand.

Dante goes around the bed and picks up the tray with food. He places it on the bed next to me.

"There has to be something on this tray that you like," he says. "You could've asked for anything, but now you only get to choose from this."

He picks up a fry off one of the plates and puts it in his mouth. I guess the food's not drugged after all, or maybe he knows exactly what isn't.

"You can't just keep me locked up in here with nothing to do," I say.

"I can do whatever the fuck I want." He grins. "Now eat something."

I let out a frustrated breath. The food is just within reach of my free hand, but I don't want to give him what he wants.

He strolls to the other end of the room and pulls out his phone. I stare at him as he leans against the wall and focuses his attention completely on the phone.

When he looks straight at me, a smile stretches across his lip. "What? You can't keep your eyes off me? You'd have my cock stuffed in your mouth again rather than food?"

I grunt, averting my gaze.

I hate him.

I hate him so fucking much.

"You can have my cock for dessert," he says.

I don't know how much time passes, but Dante is busy with his phone and obviously enjoying the whole thing, and I'm so angry because I know negotiating with him is impossible right now.

What is he going to do if I keep refusing to do what he wants me to?

I want to keep fighting him, but I have a problem.

I've drunk too much water to try to chase away my hunger, and now I really have to pee. But I'm cuffed to the bed and can't go to the bathroom.

I look at Dante, but he doesn't lift his gaze to me, even though he has to be aware of me staring at him.

"Can you get this off?" I ask, shaking my hand with the cuff. "I need to use the bathroom."

"You're not going anywhere until you eat."

"But I—"

"If you can't hold it, that's not my problem."

I grit my teeth. "I'm serious. I really need to go."

"Then go." He flashes me a quick smile before returning his attention to his phone.

Ugh! Why does he have so much free time to be here? Why does he want to be here? I guess he just likes messing with me.

I think about my options, and I don't really have any. This isn't how I'm going to achieve anything, is it?

I'm already cuffed to the bed. He's just going to force-feed me if he wants to. I'll have to find another way.

I pick up a piece of toast and put it in my mouth. My stomach groans immediately as the delicious taste fills my mouth.

I swallow, barely able to contain myself from grabbing all the food off the tray and devouring it. Now that I've tasted it, it's impossible to stop thinking about it or ignore my hunger.

"Slow down. You're going to make yourself sick," Dante says, and when I look up at him, I catch a glimpse of something in his eyes.

A tiny sparkle of warmth in all that cold.

Or maybe it's just a shadow.

I take a deep breath, willing myself to take smaller, slower bites.

Even though I hate to admit it, he's right. If I just gobble it all up, like I want to, I'm going to throw it all up.

When I'm done, I tug at the cuff, making it clink to get Dante's attention. He slips his phone back into his pocket and strides to me.

"You're going to eat every meal that's brought to you." His eyes lock on mine. "Or we're going to have a problem. And you don't want to piss me off." He lowers his hand to my neck, but his touch is strangely gentle, which somehow scares me even more. "I won't always find your disobedience entertaining. You can go now."

When he lets go of me, he unlocks the cuffs. I rub my wrist, staring at the red marks the cuff has left.

I push myself up and crawl to the other side of the bed so I don't have to pass too close to him.

But once I reach the bathroom and want to close the door, he catches it. I glance at him over my shoulder.

"The door stays open," he says, and my jaw hits the floor.

"What? But I—"

He holds the door open, his eyes daring me to try to argue with him. If I do, he's just going to tell me I don't have to use the bathroom, isn't he?

I shoot him a glare and angrily stride inside. He leans on the door as I do my best to get my panties down without him seeing too much.

As if he hasn't already seen and touched too much.

The whole thing seems to amuse him even more, and I feel my face warming up.

I do my best to ignore him.

Why is he doing this to me?

Did he think I'd try to throw up what I ate?

I have no idea, but he clearly wants me alive for now. Maybe I can use that somehow, but I'm not sure how.

At least not yet.

CHAPTER 8

I EAT ALL THE DAMN FOOD ELENA BRINGS ME. IT MAKES ME feel a bit better. Stronger. My mind is less hazy too.

Dante doesn't show up for days. I have no idea where he is or what he's doing. Maybe he's not even in the house.

"Ma'am," Elena says, and I look up at her in surprise. "It's time for your walk."

My eyebrows shoot up. "My walk?"

"Yes, ma'am. You need some fresh air."

I blink at her, wondering if I'm hallucinating and there was something in my food after all.

But Elena is still standing there, waiting for me.

I'm getting out of this damn room.

It's the only thing I can think about. I've done what Dante wants me to do and now I got something.

A tiny concession.

Even prisoners have some rights, I suppose.

"Um, okay. I'm ready." I straighten my dress and slip on my shoes.

"Follow me, please," she says, eyeing me carefully before disappearing through the door.

When I step out into the hallway, I expect Dante to be there and laugh at me for tricking me into thinking that I'd be allowed out.

But it's only the guards who are waiting for me.

A whole lot of them.

Shit.

Anything's better than being trapped in my room, and even squished between the guards, I should be able to see something that I might find useful for my escape.

The guards lead me down the hallway and downstairs. I try to memorize my surroundings as much as possible, but the whole thing doesn't give me much hope.

The exit is too far away, and there are more guards posted everywhere. This place is like a fucking fortress, which means that even if I somehow slip out of my room, getting past all the guards will be almost impossibly hard.

But now that I'm allowed to go out, maybe I can find another way to escape. The guards are watching my every step and my every move, but that doesn't mean they won't relax around me eventually.

Even though I'm impatient to get away from here, I know I can't make any rash moves.

I need to convince everyone, including Dante, that I'm not going to be a problem or try to run away again. Once they stop thinking about me too much, I might be able to find a way.

The guards take me behind the house, to a huge garden. There are trees and flowers everywhere, and the grass is soft under my shoes.

I take a deep breath. Fresh air fills my lungs, and this is so much better than just standing next to an open window.

The guards give me some space, and it looks like now they're following me where I decide to go rather than leading me around.

I keep going, studying my surroundings. But that only gets me more frustrated because I can't see much.

It's just endless fields and trees. How am I supposed to know in which direction to go? If I follow the road, they'll find me very quickly.

Once again, I have regrets about my old life. I should've gotten a driver's license or at least learned how to drive.

Maybe a friend from college could've helped me. Then I could find a way to steal one of the cars parked in the parking lot and get myself out of here.

But no.

I can't do it.

Because it never crossed my mind that I might need something like that. My father's driver always took me wherever I needed to go, and I didn't have to think about transportation.

If only I'd worried more about my freedom than about trying to impress and please my father.

Maybe someone has a bike around here. Surprisingly, I know how to ride a bike. One of my private tutors taught me how to do it when I was a kid.

As I get to the other side of the house, I spot a pool. When I go closer, my mouth falls open.

Dante is there.

Shirtless.

And doing crunches.

His gaze finds mine and he flashes me a smile. After he jumps to his feet, he makes his way to me. I don't know if I should stay where I am or try to walk away.

"Wife," he says, brushing his fingers over my cheek.

The touch sends a current through me, and I jerk away from him.

My gaze briefly falls to his perfect abs. I don't want to stare, but my eyes go lower anyway.

His pants hang low on his hips, and I don't like where my mind is going or what I'm picturing, and I especially don't want to feel a spark inside me, so I force my gaze away.

As if Dante can read my thoughts, a smile curves his lips. "You just can't stay away from me."

"I wasn't looking for you." I cross my arms.

And really, it's not my fault he just happened to be here.

"Sir!" A man runs to Dante with a phone in his hand. "A call for you!"

Dante's face grows serious as he steps away from me and takes the phone. "Who?"

"Your uncle."

Dante's fingers curl around the phone before he answers. "Hello, uncle." His voice is clipped.

I wonder if he wants me to go away, but he doesn't say anything, so I and the guards just stand there.

If he doesn't want me to overhear anything, I'm sure he'll order me to leave, but maybe he doesn't care about what I hear because he doesn't believe I'll ever get a chance to use any of it against him.

"Yeah, I married the Verratti girl. What do you care?" Dante says.

They're talking about me.

I don't know why his uncle cares either, and I'd like to know, but I don't have super hearing to be able to hear what is being said on the other end of the line.

Dante laughs.

It's one of his chilling laughs that probably mean he's not amused at all.

"Seriously? You've got to be fucking kidding me. She's my wife. Mine."

Is this really all about me?

Dante glances at me. "I don't give a fuck about what you want. If you wanted to make a deal with the Verrattis yourself, you could have. But oh, wait, I forgot. You don't really have anything to offer. They realized it too. I don't know what the hell you're trying to achieve now, but forget it. It's not going to work."

I guess it's not really about me, but more about what I represent. They're probably discussing me as if I'm a house they both want to own because they can benefit from it.

I have no clue what Dante's uncle may be suggesting. It's not like Dante is going to divorce me so he can give me to him.

But there's probably something else I don't know about because Dante is silent as he listens to what his uncle has to say.

"No deal," he finally says. "And if you set foot in my territory, you're a dead man. Do you hear me?"

He ends the call and turns to the guy who brought him the phone. "Tell everyone that if they see my uncle or any of his men in my territory, they have my permission to take them out."

"Yes, sir." The guy inclines his head.

Dante turns to me, and his face is completely

expressionless now, his eyes cold and empty. "Take my wife back to her room," he says to the guards.

Shit.

I don't want to go back to that damn room so soon, but if I try to argue with him now that he's clearly bothered by whatever his uncle has offered, I probably won't get another chance to go out.

I follow the guards back to the house.

Back to my prison.

My freedom is still far, far away, but maybe I can come up with a decent plan eventually. I just have to make sure I don't lose my mind first.

CHAPTER 9

I STARE THROUGH THE WINDOW, TRYING TO IGNORE THE bars, but it's impossible.

It's raining outside again, and it's been raining for a few days now, which means I haven't left my room for a while.

When I turn away from the window, my thoughts fly back to Dante. It must be nice to be free to do whatever the hell he wants. I don't know where he is, but for some reason, I picture him in some fancy room as he takes off his clothes.

I blink.

What the fuck?

I don't know why I'm even thinking about him like that when I should be thinking about my plan so I can get the hell out of here.

But I've been thinking about that for hours now, and I

haven't really come up with anything, so why not get my mind off everything for a bit?

Maybe it'll help me brainstorm eventually.

Yeah right.

Who am I kidding?

Dante is incredibly hot, and I hate that he is who he is, because it would've been so nice if we'd met at college or at a bar.

Hell, I would've found a way around my father's men just to meet up with him. There weren't any hot guys in my classes. Not even any hot professors.

I run my hand over my face.

Gah! I'm already losing my mind because I'm locked up in here.

How else can I explain all these weird thoughts I have about Dante? Even if he weren't a mafia boss, he'd still probably be a jerk.

A handsome jerk, but a jerk anyway.

I hear footsteps in the hallway, so I listen carefully.

A few moments later, the door opens. Elena enters the room, and I furrow my brow because instead of a tray with food, she's carrying a box.

She places the box on the bed.

"You need to put this on, ma'am," she says. "I'll be back in five minutes."

When she leaves, I go closer to inspect the box. It's big and white. I open it.

A dress.

There's a black dress in the box, and I grit my teeth when I spread it out. It's fucking see-through and looks as if a bunch of black flowers were placed together.

If I put it on, I'll feel like wearing nothing. The material is so thin and flimsy, and there's a slit on the side that goes so high up I'm sure everyone will be able to see my underwear when I move.

It seems tight too, like a second skin, and my breasts would be on display because of the deep V-cut.

Why the hell does anyone think I'd like to wear something like that?

But of course, they don't.

What I think or feel doesn't matter.

I bet it's Dante who wants to see me in this thing. It's not like there's anyone else who'd have a say in it.

He probably picked it himself, and I don't even know why. It's not like I'm going anywhere.

I tightly grip the dress in my fingers, all the anger I've been bottling up for days coming to the surface.

Letting out a low growl, I tear at the dress.

After a few strong tugs, the material rips. I want to scream as I keep ripping the dress until the only thing left is a pile of material on my bed.

I throw the box across the room too. I'm not Dante's puppet, and I refuse to play whatever game he's playing now.

When Elena opens the door, her gaze falls on me and then on the bed. Her lips part in surprise, a little gasp escaping her throat. She immediately closes the door and locks it again.

I sit on the bed and lower my head into my hands. I feel a little bit better now, but not much.

When the door flies open, I jerk back and look up.

Dante.

I expect to see fury on his face and in his eyes, but instead, I see nothing.

Blank.

His face gives me nothing as he just stands there, his gaze going from me and then to the dress, or what's left of it.

"What did you do?" he asks, and his calm tone chills me.

Him being so collected and emotionless is scarier than his anger.

"I'm not a doll you can just play dress-up with," I say.

He tilts his head. "And that's why you ruined a perfectly good dress?"

"It wasn't a dress. It was worse than lingerie."

"You didn't even try it on. It would've looked breathtaking on you." The corners of his lips lift up, and I don't like his smile at all. "But maybe it's better you ruined it because now I get to punish you."

"What are you going to do?" I glare at him. "Lock me up? Oh wait, I'm already locked up!"

He crosses the room and grabs my arm, pulling me to my feet. I try to back away from him, but he's too strong.

Before I can do or say anything, he sits on the bed, tugs me to him, and I find myself across his lap.

I thrash, but somehow, he catches my wrists and pins them at the small of my back and his leg traps both of mine.

"I'm going to spank you," he says.

A thrill I don't expect rushes between my legs.

I wiggle, but I can't free myself.

I'm trapped, completely at his mercy.

And the worst part is, I think I like it.

"Stay still," he orders.

When I don't comply, he smacks my ass hard, making me gasp.

I freeze when I feel him lift my dress up. He rubs my ass through my panties, and heat pools low in my stomach.

Why the hell does this turn me on so much?

His fingers trail down to my pussy, pressing and probing, and I'm wet in an instant.

But then he hooks his fingers into the waistband of my panties and pulls them down, exposing me to him.

His erection pokes my stomach through his pants,

and I wiggle once again, but this time I'm not sure what I'm actually doing.

I want to rub myself against something.

His hand, maybe.

I want him to touch me.

I want his fingers to play with my clit again.

When he brings his hand down on my bottom, I'm surprised by the intensity of it and the sting.

A yelp escapes me when his hand collides with my cheeks over and over again in quick succession.

His smacks are hard and merciless, and my skin is getting warmer and more tender. But every time his palm connects with my flesh, I also feel a tingle between my legs.

I cry out when a flurry of smacks hits the back of my thighs, and I hate that my need is only getting stronger.

When Dante releases me, I don't move. I'm too confused by the sensations that are spreading through my body that I don't even know what I'm supposed to do.

Dante runs his fingers over my burning cheeks, and I push my hips against his hand, wanting his fingers to explore my wetness.

But instead of doing what I want, Dante lifts me up and moves me onto the bed.

Then he gets up and goes for the door without another word.

I stare after him, my body screaming with desire.

Is he really just going to leave now?

I can see the bulge in his pants as he turns to look at me from the door. He clearly wants more too, so why is he denying himself?

His jaw tightens, and for a few moments, he just stands there in the doorway, as if he's about to change his mind.

As if he's angry, but not with me.

Himself, maybe.

But then he steps out and closes the door behind him.

I throw myself on the bed, staring at the ceiling and trying to ignore the throbbing between my legs.

It takes a while for the pressure to dissipate.

I should be glad Dante left. Who knows what he wants to do to me? Maybe I wouldn't like it at all.

Why would I even want him to touch me?

I should be disgusted.

Embarrassed too.

He saw just how turned on I was, and now he probably thinks that he can play me the way he wants. Maybe I did exactly what he wanted after all.

Again, I ask myself why he left.

Does it bother him that he was turned on too? But I don't know why he did what he did then.

Did he expect a different result? Was he hoping that the whole thing would do nothing for him?

Was he trying to show me that everything he does is deliberate and that he won't just lose control?

I close my eyes and groan.

Maybe everything is just a game to him. Maybe he enjoys controlling me and tormenting me, and leaving me wanting.

He can quench his thirst with whomever and wherever he wants, and I can't.

I can only get more frustrated and fantasize about things that won't happen.

I hate Dante now more than ever.

I hate him so much I want to cry.

But I can't let him break me or mess with my mind.

I can't.

CHAPTER 10

I don't see Dante for days, and I don't get out of my room.

It's getting harder and harder to think about escaping because my mind is asking all the wrong questions instead. I wonder about Dante too much.

I want to get to know him better. Even though I keep saying to myself that it's because I want to gather as much info as possible so I can escape him, I'm not sure that's the only reason.

Dante is a mystery, and since I don't have anything to do, all I can think about is unraveling it.

Maybe he's grown bored of me, or maybe he isn't even here. He could've gone off somewhere on business or for pleasure.

I clench my jaw.

For some reason, the idea that Dante might've gone

to someone else for pleasure makes me annoyed. I guess I'm just envious that he's free, and I'm not.

And I've come up with nothing to get away.

But maybe there's a way I can get out of this room or at least find out if Dante is here.

I get off the bed and look around the room. There's not much here I can destroy, but I can try.

A little voice in my head is telling me I shouldn't provoke the beast, but if I don't do something, I feel like I'm going to lose my mind.

I think about everything that's happened.

My life at college.

My family.

My marriage to Dante.

And just like that, my anger bubbles up. I yank the covers off the bed and throw the pillows across the room.

I pick up the tray with empty plates and chuck it at the nearest wall. There's a loud crashing sound as the broken pieces fall everywhere.

I go to the closet and pull everything out of it, spilling it all over the floor. After I kick one of the shoes that fell out, I grab the curtains and tug hard until they fall off.

I'm so busy with my rampage that I don't hear the door open and someone coming in until they grab me from behind.

I manage to spin around and find myself face-to-face with Dante.

His eyes are glistening with an emotion I can't recognize in the moonlight, and the look on his face scares me.

He grabs my wrists and shoves me against the wall. The impact forces a gasp out of my throat.

Dante pins my wrists above my head, trapping me with his body.

"What the fuck are you doing?" he asks. "Have you lost your mind?"

I try to push him off me, but it's impossible.

"What do you think?" I snap. "It's what you want, isn't it? That's why you keep me caged in here like some kind of animal!"

When his gaze lowers to my lips, I see how dangerously close his face is to mine. His eyes lock on mine, and for a few long moments, we don't move or say anything, just stare at each other.

Half of his face is in darkness now, but even though I'm scared, there's also something else.

He dips his face toward mine, our lips almost brushing.

Whatever thought I might've had, it's gone now.

All I can feel is his body pressed against mine and the heat traveling through my body.

Dante's breathing quickens, as if I'm fighting him.

But I'm not.

I'm perfectly still, just waiting to see what he's going to do.

It's him who's fighting something.

Something I can't see.

A growl leaves his throat as he presses his forehead against mine.

"What is it about you?" he whispers, and I don't know if he's asking me or himself.

He lifts his head and looks at me.

I focus on his mouth a moment before his lips crash against mine. His mouth hungrily ravages mine, and my lips respond, as if we've kissed a thousand times before.

One of his hands lowers down my arm and roughly kneads my breast, igniting a fire inside me.

I let out a soft moan as his hand moves down, and he shifts so his fingers can sneak under my dress.

His eyes briefly meet mine, and I don't even have to tell him anything. He knows I don't want him to stop, just like I can tell he doesn't want to stop either.

Lifting me up in his arms, he brings his lips back to mine, and I wrap myself around him as he carries me to the bed.

Something crunches under his shoes, but he doesn't seem to care. I'm just glad I at least left the sheets on the bed.

He unzips my dress before lowering me onto the bed.

I watch him as he jerks his shirt over his head and

throws it aside. The strong muscles of his chest and arms flex as he climbs on top of me.

His lips collide with mine as his fingers bury in my dress. He yanks it down my body and I hear it hit the floor.

His mouth shifts to my neck, and he leaves a bunch of kisses all over my collarbone.

He grips my bra so hard that I hear the material rip, and he easily tosses it away too. When his mouth closes around my nipple, I let out a groan.

A billion different sensations course through my body as his hand cups my other breast.

He pinches my nipple just as his teeth graze the other, and I can't think about anything anymore, just the delicious pricks of pain mixing with an even more intense pleasure.

He tortures and plays with my breasts, sucking and squeezing, and my need only grows stronger. His eyes lift to mine as his lips trail a path down my stomach.

He grasps my panties and almost tears them off me too. When there's nothing covering me anymore, he pushes himself up and his hungry gaze explores my body, as if he wants to memorize every curve.

I bite down on my lip as I lift my knees and spread my legs wide for him. If that's not enough of an invitation for him, I don't know what is.

He grips my thighs, his fingers digging into my skin, and then he buries his face between my legs.

His tongue glides over my pussy and pushes inside.

I try to lift my hips toward his mouth, but he's still tightly holding my thighs. His tongue flicks over my clit as he sucks on my tender flesh.

My breath comes out in little gasps as he laps at me and my whole body trembles with pleasure.

A few twists of his tongue push me over the edge, and I let out a loud cry as my release pulses through me.

Dante lets go of me, pushing himself up, and watches me as I'm trying to catch my breath. He unzips his pants and yanks them down, along with his underwear.

His cock springs out, and my eyes widen a little because of how hard and big he is. As he climbs back on the bed, a tiny pang of fear fills my stomach.

Will it hurt?

But Dante runs his fingers up and down my legs, and my desire overpowers everything else. He positions himself between my legs while caressing my skin, his eyes trained on me.

When the tip of him grazes my entrance, I tense. He rubs himself against me until my muscles relax, and then he shoves himself inside me.

There's a very brief moment of pain, but it's soon replaced by the sensation of him filling and stretching me.

He pulls out and dives back in, and a moan steals its way out of my mouth.

I like it.

I like the feeling of his body against mine as he leans over me to place a kiss on my lips. His hands find mine, and our fingers intertwine as he keeps me pinned to the bed.

His thrusts quicken as he fucks me deep and hard, and I can barely believe how good it makes me feel. It's like my whole body is discovering all these wonderful sensations I didn't even know existed.

He pushes his hips against mine, his warm body enveloping me as he pounds into me. The whole bed shakes under us, and the sounds of our bodies connecting and my moans and Dante's grunts fill the air.

My insides throb and tingle, and as Dante slams himself inside me, I cry out and bite his shoulder. My orgasm spreads through me like a tsunami, and Dante comes a moment later with a groan.

He kisses me again, and when he pushes himself up, he glances at his shoulder where I bit him, the imprint of my teeth visible in his skin.

His eyes meet mine, and then a smile spreads across his lips as he chuckles.

"You *are* a wild animal," he teases, and I press my lips into a tight line and narrow my eyes at him before a smile breaks out on my face.

The pure bliss I'm feeling just doesn't leave any space for anything else.

Dante rolls off me and lies next to me. As I try to catch my breath, I watch his chest rapidly rise and fall.

I want to reach out to him, but I stop myself.

A few moments later, he climbs to his feet and quickly gets dressed. He glances at me before leaving, and I wish my pillow weren't on the floor because I want to place it over my head.

What the hell has just happened?

Did I let him use me for his pleasure?

Except, the pleasure was mine too.

It's just sex.

It means absolutely nothing.

We were just blowing off some steam.

Maybe if I keep repeating it, it will become true.

CHAPTER 11

THE NEXT DAY ELENA BRINGS ME FIVE BOXES AFTER SHE cleans up most of the mess. I watch her carefully as she places the last box on the bed, and I wonder what's in them.

"Master says you should pick one and put it on," she says, and my eyebrows shoot up.

So Dante still wants to dress me up for some reason, but at least now I have a choice.

Huh.

When Elena leaves, I open the boxes one by one.

Five different dresses.

Five completely different styles.

I spread them out on the bed and move the boxes to the floor so I'll have enough space. The first dress is made of black lace, but it's too sexy and sort of reminds me of the one I destroyed. So no, definitely not that one.

The second is plain and pale pink; sleeveless with a turtleneck. I don't like that one either. It seems too confining and somehow too innocent.

The third dress is red silk. It's definitely sexy, almost like a nightgown, just flowier and more comfortable looking. There's something about it that I like.

If I had to name it, I'd call it *passion*.

The fourth one is a plain dark blue cocktail dress, and it's kind of nice, but a little bit too business-like and official. If I were going to a business party, I might wear something like that.

I sigh.

If only I could go to a business party.

My mind instantly jumps to a different world where I have my degree and I can do whatever I want, including attending business parties.

Would I find them fun or boring? I guess I'll never know.

Even if I escape Dante, I'll never be able to get my degree, because if I try, he's going to find me, or my father will find me and kill me for disgracing our family.

Pushing those thoughts out of my mind, I focus on the fifth dress.

It's bright pink and very tight and short. Like something I'd want to wear to a nightclub or a college party.

If I were free to do it.

Nope, not that damn dress either.

I don't want anything to remind me of my college days, even if they were the best and happiest period of my life.

Being far enough away from my family made me forget all the drama, and I rarely even remembered I was a mafia princess unless I had to stop myself from doing something my family wouldn't approve of if they found out about it.

I end up choosing the red dress, and I go to the bathroom to change. It glides over my skin, and I wish I had a mirror, but I feel good in it, so I hope it looks fine.

When I get out of the bathroom, I nearly yelp because Elena is there. She gives me an approving look and leaves, only to return with another box, a smaller one this time.

Extending her arms, she offers the box to me. I step forward and take it. When I open it, I see a pair of red high heels that go perfectly with the dress.

I slip out of my shoes and put on the heels as Elena watches me.

Just how sharp is that heel?

I could use it to stab someone.

Dante, maybe.

Speaking of Dante... I don't really want to think about what we did last night because then I'd have to contemplate what it means, and I can't handle that right now.

"Ma'am," Elena says as she pulls a lipstick out of her pocket.

Unlike my plain black dresses, hers actually has hidden pockets. I'd be envious if I actually had some use for pockets, but I don't.

She approaches me, and I stand still as she applies the red lipstick to my lips. When she's done, I briefly smack my lips together.

A smile spreads across Elena's face.

I guess I look fine because she pockets the lipstick.

"Come with me, ma'am," she says.

Wait, am I actually going to be allowed out of the room? Wow.

I follow Elena into the hallway. The guards are waiting for us, but they let Elena and me go first and then trail after us.

Instead of taking me to the front door, Elena leads me through a hallway and into a large dining room that's bathed in golden colors. The huge table in the middle is already set up, and Dante sits at the end of it.

His lips part as his eyes take me in, and a small smile crosses his lips.

"I told you it was the one," he says to Elena.

"Yes, you did, sir." She laughs softly.

I look from her to him, wondering what they're talking about.

"Sit," Dante says, his gaze meeting mine as he points to the chair to his right.

I take a seat, glancing at him.

"You look stunning," he says, picking up a bottle of red wine.

He pours some into my glass.

"Thanks, I guess." I snatch the glass and take a sip.

The wine tastes great, and I can't help but wonder why I'm here and what Dante is planning.

Maybe I should just ask.

Elena shows up with a serving cart full of food, and as she puts the big plates and bowls on the table, the mouthwatering smell makes me instantly hungry.

"Thank you, Elena," Dante says, and she inclines her head.

When she's gone, Dante's attention is back on me.

"You can pick whatever you want," he says.

Wow, so many choices all of a sudden.

I put some mashed potatoes on my plate first, and whenever I reach for something, I can feel Dante's eyes on me.

It's slightly unnerving, and it makes me incredibly self-conscious.

It almost reminds me of all the dinners I had with my family, except Dante's gaze is nothing like the disapproving and scrutinizing gaze of my father, who was just looking for me to make a mistake so he could berate me.

A drop of red sauce falls off my spoon and onto the pristine white tablecloth. I let out a soft groan.

Just what I need.

But when I glance at Dante, he's not mad. His lips are spread into a small smile.

As I nibble on a piece of meat, I eye Dante as he serves himself.

My father always insists on having servants around during meals and he expects someone to wait on him, but I guess Dante isn't like my father.

When Dante's eyes lift to mine, I quickly look away. I don't want him to think I'm staring at him because I'm obsessed with him or something.

"Did you know you were going to be my wife?" he suddenly asks, and my head snaps to him.

Why is he asking me that?

Why does he care?

"No." I lick my lips to get a crumb off, hoping the lipstick Elena put on me isn't one of those that easily smear. "I mean, I found out a few days before."

"But you knew your family arranged a marriage for you?" His inquiring eyes are trained on mine.

"No, I didn't." Because if I had, I would've run far, far away.

His brow furrows, but I can't tell what he's thinking.

"You attended college," he says.

It's not a question, but I answer anyway. "Yeah."

"Did you like it?"

I look at him.

Is he asking because he genuinely wants to know or is he trying to rub it in my face that now I can't do anything anymore?

But all I see is the curiosity in his eyes.

"I loved it." I wait for his reaction, but he gives me nothing.

"Did you have friends?"

"Yeah, of course. And you? Did you go to college?"

He shakes his head. "It was never in the plans for me. Did you have a boyfriend?"

His question throws me off for a second, and I just stare at him.

Why would he care about that?

Unless he's concerned that he wasn't my first.

"You can tell me the truth." He must've seen my hesitation. "I won't be mad."

Except, I have no clue why he's asking, and I don't know if he'll react in the way he says he will.

It could be a trap.

But luckily, I don't have anything to hide.

"No," I say. "My father's people were always lurking somewhere and watching my every step."

"You've never been in love with someone? Not even had a small, innocent crush on someone?" He leans forward, as if he wants to rip the truth out of me, or maybe get inside my brain and read my thoughts.

It's funny, because I'd like to do the same to him.

"No. I may have lived on campus, but, at the back of my mind, I just knew who I was. Simply falling in love with someone was never going to work. If I let myself even entertain the fantasy of being with someone, I'm sure my father would've hunted him down and killed him. And maybe I don't even know what love is. In our world, people don't lead ordinary lives." I regret my words in an instant because I think I spilled too much.

"I agree."

I raise an eyebrow at him.

"It's easier for you," I say before I can stop myself. "You can have both."

"What do you mean?" He tilts his head.

"You can do whatever the hell you want, and you can have as many crushes or lovers as you want. You can even be married and have your true love by your side too. It might be a bit risky because of who you are, but if you take all the precautions, you can lead a double life without a problem."

He jerks back, surprise flashing through his eyes.

"Do you know what love is? Do you have someone out there who's willing to love someone like you? Or is it just about sex with you? Do you have a secret girlfriend who doesn't have a clue who you really are?" I should just keep my mouth shut, but I can't.

I guess I find some dark satisfaction in seeing him have a reaction to my words, and maybe I'm just curious.

His face is serious, and his gaze moves across the room.

"Matteo," he calls, getting to his feet. "It's good you're here. We should deal with that thing now."

I turn my head in the direction of the door.

Matteo stands in the doorway with a perplexed look on his face. "The thing, sir?"

"You know, that..." Dante waves his hand as if the gesture is supposed to mean something.

"Um, okay," Matteo says, but he still looks completely clueless.

Did Dante just make up something to get out of a conversation with me?

Seriously?

The big scary wolf is afraid of Little Red Riding Hood?

I'm probably imagining things.

When he and Matteo leave, the guards step into the room. I wait for them to tell me to go back to my room, but they just stand there.

It looks like I can finish my meal in peace.

As I take another bite, I wonder what exactly about my questions bothered Dante so much.

Does he actually have a lover no one knows about? Does the woman in question know what he is, or does she think he's just a regular guy and would run away screaming if she found out the truth?

Or maybe the idea has never even occurred to him.

I'm an idiot.

He probably just didn't care to waste his time answering me, and I was silly for even asking such things.

He's not capable of loving or caring about someone. All he cares about is his own pleasure. Loving someone requires emotions that he doesn't have or can understand.

And probably neither do I.

It's not like I had an example at home to learn from.

There's only been sacrifice and duty.

Nothing else.

I pick up my glass of wine and down it.

CHAPTER 12

Once I'm back in my room, I can't stop thinking about Dante and about our conversation. It still bugs me that I don't know why he reacted the way he did.

And hell, I also wonder if there's something wrong with me because I might be imagining things.

Maybe I'm seeing something that isn't there for some reason.

Maybe I'm reading too much into the situation.

There's no reason for him to care about something as trivial as love. It means nothing to him.

His life is completely focused on his business, and if he killed his father and brother in cold blood, then I can't imagine he'd care about anyone else.

And yet, I'm surprised he didn't brag about his conquests or told me that he'd fucked half of the city just because he could.

But maybe he really remembered something business-related, and I wasn't important enough to him, so he didn't bother to answer.

I roll over in the bed and grab my pillow so I can hug it to myself. My chance of escaping is getting lower every day instead of higher.

Dante might have let me out of my room, but the guards don't have anything better to do except follow me, and it's not very likely I can distract them or escape them.

They'd have to be distracted by something else, like an attack on this house, but I'm sure Dante's security would never allow it.

And if I don't escape, then what?

I chew on the inside of my cheek.

How can I get the best out of my situation?

Will Dante eventually allow me to do more things and let me leave my room on my own? Or will he offer me crumbs that are just enough so I don't go completely insane?

I keep thinking that he'll lose interest in me.

I'm still new to him now. Maybe that's why he asked about my life. Once he satisfies his curiosity, then what?

I think about the possibility that I end up like my mother. She somehow managed to convince herself that whatever she feels for my father is love, and she's clung to that delusion ever since.

Maybe it doesn't sound like a delusion to her anymore. It's all normal to her.

But I don't want that.

I don't want to have zero control over my own life.

I don't want my life to be completely devoid of emotion and affection. Maybe I haven't seen what true love looks like at home, but I've seen it in movies.

I want to be able to find out if there's really such thing as love, and I want to know what it feels like. Even if it's not the most epic thing ever, I want to be free to explore the possibility that it exists.

But maybe this whole thing is my punishment.

Maybe it's just karma hitting me back for what I did when I was younger.

My thoughts shift to my older half-sister.

I don't remember how old I was, but I know I was just a kid. My sister was a teen. Sixteen, I think.

I don't know anything about her mother, but I know my father took my half-sister from her and brought her to live with us.

It was painful to watch my mother smile and pretend she was fine with my sister living with us, but whenever my father wasn't around, her smile faded, and sometimes she cried.

I've never really understood why, since my half-sister was conceived before my parents were married, and I don't think my father was in contact with her mother after.

I wouldn't be surprised if my sister was a product of some fling, and my father only snatched her from her mother because he could use her.

Very soon, my sister ended up engaged to one of my father's business partners. He was much older than her, closer to our father's age.

Even though I didn't interact with my sister much, I knew she was upset and didn't want to marry. I mean, who would?

It was insane, and she didn't even grow up with my family. She'd only been with us for a few months and couldn't forget what the real, free world was like.

One night, I woke up because I heard a noise. When I cracked the door of my room open to see what it was, I saw my sister.

She was dressed as if she was going somewhere, and she had a backpack too. I guess she must've figured out the guards' schedule and that there was a hole in the fence around the house.

When she turned and saw me, she gasped and immediately ran over to me, begging me to stay quiet because she needed to get away from a very bad man who was supposed to become her husband.

I don't remember what I did.

I think I nodded, but when she was just down the hallway, I started running in the opposite direction—where my father's room was—and screamed for him.

All I wanted was his approval.

His affection.

For once, I wanted him to look at me and tell me I'd done the right thing. Maybe even hug me. I wanted him to be proud of me.

But once he heard what was going on, he grabbed his gun and summoned the guards. He didn't even look at me.

I suppressed a lot of what happened that night from my memory, but I know there was a lot of screaming and crying. Then the man my sister was supposed to marry came and took her away.

After that, my father was even colder and stricter with me, maybe because he believed I'd turn out like my sister otherwise.

He wanted my complete and full obedience and devotion, even if he didn't really give me anything in return.

For a long time, I didn't want to think about my sister. But now I wonder where she is and if she's still alive. I can't imagine what her life is like.

I should've never alerted my father. If she'd run away, maybe she would've saved herself. Or maybe my father would've found her.

Now there's no way to know.

I can't even tell her that I'm sorry and that I was just a stupid kid.

My apology probably wouldn't mean anything to her now.

I'm angry with myself again for burying this so deep inside my mind that I didn't even consider it when I was supposed to.

I didn't just damn my sister, but I damned myself too. I guess I've always known that I did the wrong thing, but not thinking about it was helping me deal with my guilt.

But maybe it's still not too late.

Even if it feels like I should abandon my dreams of freedom and just accept the situation because it's what I deserve, and there's barely any hope that I'll get away, I shouldn't just give up.

I can't.

If I simply accept things as they are, I'll be no better than my mother, and I hated seeing what her life was like every day.

No, I have to find a way.

No matter what it takes.

I'm not my mother.

I'm not my sister.

I'm not that child who hoped her daddy would hug her and tell her she did something right.

I'm me.

And for as long as I remember that, there will still be a lot of fight left in me.

CHAPTER 13

I haven't seen Dante for a few days, but I heard some whispers in the hallway that he won a small fight against his uncle.

When the door of my room opens, I expect to see Elena.

But instead, Dante stands in the doorway, a paper bag in his hand.

A smile stretches across his lips, and I can see he's in a good mood because his shoulders are relaxed and his eyes seem a tiny bit less cold.

I guess the whispers were right. He's won something.

I wonder if he had to kill anyone to achieve it, so he's happy because his bloodlust was satisfied, but I push that thought away.

"Hello, wife," he says as he enters, offering the bag to me. "I have something for you."

I take the bag and peek inside.

A bunch of bikinis?

"Pick one that you like and put it on," he says. "But if you don't like any and you prefer to be naked, I won't mind."

"Why?" I eye him carefully.

"Because you're hot." He grins.

I scowl. "No, not that. Why do I need a bikini?"

"You'll see." He winks at me and goes to the door. "I'll be back. Don't take too long."

I have no idea what he's planning or what he wants.

Out of all the bikinis, I take a plain black one that's not too revealing.

As I'm getting undressed in the bathroom, I think about Dante again. He could've sent Elena to bring this to me, but he didn't. He came himself.

Why?

When I'm dressed, I look down my body and furrow my brow.

The bikini is nice and covers me fine, but will I have to walk through the house like this, where the guards can see me?

I know they're supposed to pretend they're not really there most of the time, but I don't think they won't stare, and I'm not sure if I'll feel comfortable with that.

My thoughts seem slightly unreasonable to me. It's

not like I'm naked, and even if we go to the pool outside, the guards will still see me there too.

But it just doesn't seem the same. Being in a bikini around Dante, who's in his suit, and the guards, who are fully dressed too, in the house is weird.

Somehow, it makes me feel vulnerable.

Maybe Dante wants to show me off like an exhibit.

I like that thought even less.

My father sometimes insisted on my mother dressing sexy so he could show her off to his friends. I remember when I took a peek from the stairway at a party that my father threw at our house and that I wasn't allowed to go anywhere near, which only made me more curious about it.

My mother was the only woman, in a flimsy dress, surrounded by a bunch of men in suits who looked like sharks that could smell blood.

She was smiling, but the way they were all looking at her... like she was a piece of meat.

I shudder and shake that thought away.

When I get out of the bathroom, Dante is there.

He's holding a black bathrobe. His eyes linger on my body before meeting mine.

"You'll need this," he says, and the tension leaves my shoulders.

I let him help me put it on, and then he offers me his

hand. I'm so surprised that I take his hand without thinking.

As he leads me out of the room, I can't stop wondering why he's doing this. Why is he being so... nice, I guess?

It's slightly disconcerting.

If he's not pretending for some reason, then I'm seeing a different side of him.

A side I didn't think he had.

When we're in the hallway, the guards are there, but I'm with Dante now, so they stay farther away and I feel less like a dangerous prisoner.

We don't go outside.

Instead, Dante takes me to the other part of the house where I've never been before. The guards open the door for us, and we find ourselves in a room with a hot tub.

I glance at Dante, who smiles at me and lets go of my hand.

He waves at the guards, and they leave the room and close the door.

Dante and I are alone. He pulls his shirt over his head, and I try not to drool too much.

When he takes off his pants, I force my gaze away.

I shrug out of my robe and Dante heads to a small table in the corner of the room. He returns with two glasses of champagne and hands one to me.

"Are you celebrating something?" I ask before taking a sip.

"Maybe. Come."

He helps me get in the tub.

The water is just the right amount of warm, and my muscles instantly relax.

But when Dante settles next to me, I realize just how small the tub is. His leg brushes mine, and a jolt of electricity shoots through me.

We sit there in silence for a few moments, sipping on our drinks.

"If you could do anything right now, what would you do?" he suddenly asks. "What's your biggest wish? Aside from my demise."

He grins, and I let out a small laugh.

He keeps an expectant look on me, waiting for my answer.

"I'd go back to college." I opt for the truth. "Once finished, I'd get a job. Hopefully, my career would progress well, and then I'd get myself an apartment somewhere nice. It doesn't have to be big or anything special, but I'd want something mine. A safe place. I'd like to be happy too."

Dante's face turns pensive. "Sounds good."

"Really?" I cock my head at him. "If you find the idea so attractive, you can leave all this behind and lead a calm life."

"It's not that simple. I have my business to take care of. You can't just walk away from that."

"I know it's not easy, but you could try. You could get a regular job somewhere. Far away from here. Get a new identity. Start over."

He chuckles. "No regular jobs pay as well as this or give as much power."

"But are money and power worth dying for?" I keep my gaze on his. "Are they worth the risk?"

"Ah, but the risk is exactly what makes it exciting. There are a billion ways to die, for all people. I'd rather live this life. Besides, it's in my blood. I can't change who I am."

"Are you sure about that?"

His brow furrows, his shoulders tensing. "My family has been in this business for decades. I was raised to be who I am now."

"So what? You can break the tradition. You can be anything you want now. At least you have the option not to be what your family intended you to be."

"The world doesn't work that way, princess," he says. "The fairytales you come up with in your pretty head aren't real. And I don't want to do anything else."

When his arm snakes around me, I realize just how close I've gotten to him without even noticing.

It just feels so damn natural.

Like his arm is right where it should be.

"I heard people talk about your uncle," I say, wondering if he'll be willing to tell me something more.

"What did you hear?" He eyes me with suspicion.

"That you made a move against him and won. Is that true?"

"Yeah." His voice is clipped. "But it was just one fight."

I'm about to ask another question when Dante's phone rings. He lets out a groan and pulls away from me.

As he gets up, I realize I could watch water drip down his body the whole fucking day. So fucking hot.

He digs through his clothes for his phone, and when he sees the screen, he presses his lips into a tight line.

When he answers, he turns away from me.

"What?" he snaps at someone on the other end of the line. "Can it wait? I'm in the middle of something."

He rubs the back of his neck and glances over his shoulder at me.

"Okay. I'll deal with it." He lowers the phone.

"You can stay here for as long as you want," he says to me as he's getting dressed.

"Why do you have to go?" I ask.

"I have to handle a situation. Purge a rat's nest."

I frown.

I know he doesn't mean actual rats. He means people.

Good moments never last too long, do they?

He's going to kill someone.

Sure, they might be bad people, but what do I know? When I'm with him, it's so easy to forget who and what he is.

Actually, *forget* isn't really the right word.

I don't forget.

I just... I don't know. I guess I get comfortable around him and feel like his business isn't a huge part of his personality and that he can easily be someone else too.

Someone I might even—

Nope, I can't think about him like that.

I can't like someone like him.

Sure, he's hot, and he knows how to make my body sing with pleasure, but that means nothing.

I'm still his prisoner.

Dante's gaze lingers on me as if he's trying to memorize every detail of my face, and then he leaves.

A part of me wonders what will happen if he doesn't return.

CHAPTER 14

A THUD WAKES ME UP.

It's still dark, but there's some illumination coming from the lights that are outside the house so the guards are able to see what's going on.

I listen carefully, my pulse speeding up.

Someone's in the hallway.

Maybe it's just one of the guards, or maybe it's someone else. I doubt someone has broken in.

If there was an attack, I would be hearing way more than just an occasional thud and footsteps.

I strain my ears some more.

Since no gunshots can be heard, I think I'm safe.

The click of the door makes me tense. The door opens and closes.

I sit up.

Dante stumbles toward me.

"Shit. Did I wake you?" he mumbles.

"What are you doing?" I ask.

"I don't know." He climbs on the bed and settles next to me. "I don't know why I'm here."

The two top buttons of his white dress shirt are open, and his sleeves are rolled up. He smells like a mix of alcohol and the scent that's unique to him.

Even in the dark, I can see the turmoil in his eyes.

"What's wrong?" I ask.

"Everything."

I look at him, wondering what he means. "I thought you were happy. Did something bad happen when you—"

"It's my uncle. Again." He sighs.

"What's up with your uncle? What is he doing now?"

"He found an ally. Someone powerful and crazy enough to dare to go against me. Before, all my uncle had were empty threats. He'd pull off some shit, like stealing my drug or weapon shipments, or he'd tip off the cops when he found out some things, or even had one of his construction companies bid for the same job as me just to spite me. But now, it looks like there's going to be a war. He's becoming a serious threat. A threat I'll have to eliminate."

"Is that a problem?" I lick my dry lips. "I mean, do you not want to kill him?"

He doesn't answer, just stares at the ceiling.

"How many people have you killed so far?" I don't know why I ask, but I guess I'm curious.

"Too many to count." His head turns to me. "Why?"

"I thought you'd keep count."

"Do you think killing is fun? That I should keep score? As if it were a sport?"

"No, I don't. But why do you do it then?"

"Because I have to. It's part of the job. It's necessary. I don't enjoy it."

I lift my eyebrows. That's definitely not something I've heard about him. I heard the opposite, actually.

"Can't you come to an agreement with your uncle?" I ask. "If you don't want to go to war with him, then find common ground."

"I can't."

"Why not? Have you tried talking to him about it? It might seem impossible right now, but maybe it's not. Maybe he'll be willing to listen to you. Does he want your territory or something?"

"Oh, he wants everything. He wants everything that's mine." His eyes bore into mine.

"Doesn't he have his own territory? Wouldn't controlling a very large area be difficult? Maybe he's not thinking about—"

"He has his territory, but it's not about that. It's because of what I did. He'll never forgive me. He's only going after me now because he wants vengeance."

I furrow my brow, wondering what he's talking about, but then I remember. "Because you..." I hesitate, unsure if I should say it out loud.

"Because I killed my father—his brother—and my own brother—his nephew," he says it so easily, without regret or any emotion.

I want to tug the covers to myself even more, but he's lying on them, so I can't.

"Why did you do it?" My voice is barely louder than a whisper.

"Because if I hadn't done it, they would've killed me. I'd been waiting for the moment to free myself from them for years. My father always pitted me against my brother."

"I didn't know."

"No one did. They still don't know. I haven't told anyone. No one knows about the games my father played with my brother and me. He'd turn everything into a competition. Every single little thing. It didn't matter to him that my brother was three years older and stronger than me. He'd force us to fight, wrestle, race against each other... He'd give us tests like in school, except they were all prepared for my brother's level and not mine. He didn't care that I wasn't taught calculus at all. He wanted me to ace the test anyway. If I dared to say it was unfair, he'd stop whatever we were doing and declare my brother the winner because, according to him, I was whining too much and he was disgusted by my weakness. He even let my brother cheat, pretending it was my fault, but he never allowed me to do the same."

My eyes go wide. That sounds absolutely horrible and cruel.

"The winner got a reward, and the loser was punished. I don't know how many times my father beat me for losing, and then he ordered my brother to do it too. My brother enjoyed it and he always laughed at me and looked for ways to humiliate me, especially because I wasn't allowed to defend myself. If I tried, they'd start all over again. Sometimes, they locked me up, naked and bleeding, in the pitch-black darkness of a small, empty, cold room in the basement, and they left me there without any food or water for hours, maybe even a couple of days."

He's staring at the ceiling, and I can see in his eyes that the memories are still fresh. They're part of the darkness I've always seen in his gaze but wasn't sure what it was before tonight.

"My father kept saying he was trying to make me strong, but it was bullshit. I knew he preferred my brother, and that if I didn't do something about it, things would never change or would only get worse for me. I waited for my moment.

"I waited for them to lower their guard around

me and think they defeated me, and then I struck. They didn't see it coming. I put so many bullets in them," the corners of his lips pull up into a smile that doesn't reach his eyes, "it looked like I was trying to make Swiss cheese out of them. After everything they did to me, watching them die was so damn satisfying. I guess what I told you wasn't completely true. I only enjoyed killing that one time. But my happiness was brief. When the adrenaline wore off, I didn't really feel any better. At least I was free."

I don't know what to say. My hand reaches out for his, and he looks at me in surprise when I intertwine my fingers with his.

"That's awful." I can't imagine going through something like that.

It's incredible he survived all of it. Doing that takes a whole lot of strength, persistence, and patience.

If I were him, I guess I would've done the same. His father and brother were monsters. There's no excuse for what they did. I used to think Dante had it all and that his life has been easy, way easier than mine, but I was wrong.

I press myself closer to him.

Maybe I want to comfort him, or I just crave his warmth. He's given me a whole new insight into his life, and I'm glad he shared his secret with me.

"What if you tell your uncle what you just told me?" I say softly.

"Won't work. He won't believe me. My father made sure no one knew. It was always just him and my brother against me. He'd explain away my bruises and broken bones as accidents, and he threatened me so I'd lie too. But enough about them and my uncle. I don't want to talk about them anymore."

"Okay. Then we'll talk about something else."

"I should go." He makes a move to get up, but I tug him and he lets me pull him back.

"No." I don't think he should be alone right now, and I don't want to be alone either.

He shifts onto his side and looks at me, his fingers brushing my cheek. The small contact sends a wave of electricity through me.

"You're so beautiful," he says.

A grin breaks out on my lips. "Did you expect me to be ugly, before you saw me?"

"I wasn't expecting anything because I didn't marry to get a wife. I did it because it was the only way your father would agree to my business proposal. It was just a too good opportunity to pass up. Even my father knew it, because he was the one who initiated it. I just finished it and tweaked it a little bit."

"Will my father's men fight with you if there's a war?" I bite down on my lip.

"No. Our deal has some conditions. He and I only fight together if our joint business is affected. It's a good deal because I have a new route for my shipments that's safe, despite being in a different country. It would take too many resources to protect it on my own. My uncle is smart, so he's only attacking my business here. I guess he knows the terms of the deal."

His gaze focuses on my lips, and he leans toward me, his mouth brushing mine.

I press my lips against his, and his kiss turns hungrier. His tongue explores my mouth, and I feel warmth spreading all over me.

He pulls away from me. "If I keep kissing you, I'll end up fucking you."

I meet his gaze. "Then keep kissing me."

Surprise flashes through his eyes, but only for a second. His mouth collides with mine, and he buries his fingers in my hair.

His kiss burns with passion and desire, and I melt into it, wanting more.

He grabs the covers and throws them off me. His gaze focuses on my body. I'm only wearing my underwear.

I like the way he's looking at me.

As if he can't get enough.

As if he's fascinated by me.

His hands roam up and down my body, and his lips

fasten to my neck. I'm already burning with a fire that's impossible to ignore, and I reach for his shirt so I can unbutton it.

He realizes what I want to do, and he just yanks at his shirt, popping the buttons. I trail my fingers down his strong chest, but he catches my hand and pins it against the bed.

As he kisses me, his hand dips down my stomach and into my panties. His fingers slide into my wetness, and I let out a moan.

His touch and his kisses scorch me, and I don't even know how and when it happens, but when I return to my senses, we're both completely naked, and Dante's mouth is making its way down my stomach.

His mouth grazes my opening, and my arousal doubles. He teases me with his tongue, and then, without warning, he flips me over onto my stomach.

He grips my hips, pulling my ass up and forcing my legs apart. His body envelops mine as he leans over me, catching my wrists.

"Now I'm going to fuck you," he whispers into my ear, his hard cock pressed against my ass, and a shudder of anticipation runs down my spine.

He rubs himself against my opening, holding my wrists trapped against the small of my back.

And then he slams himself inside me.

A groan escapes my throat.

He slaps my ass as he pumps in and out of me, his grip on my wrists tightening.

He buries his cock so deep inside me that it feels like we're one body instead of two. I push my hips against his, meeting his forceful thrusts, as he smacks my ass again.

My body throbs with all kinds of wonderful sensations as he fucks me hard and fast.

I gasp when he lets go of my wrists and his fingers tangle in my hair instead. He presses my head down while he pounds into me, and then he yanks at my hair, forcing me up, so I end up sitting on his lap.

He keeps moving inside me as he winds his arms tightly around me, his hands roughly kneading and pinching my breasts, his mouth grazing my earlobe.

"Come for me," he whispers into my ear, and sucks on my earlobe as his cock impales me.

The pleasure inside me explodes, and I cry out and briefly close my eyes, losing myself in his embrace.

His release follows, and he pulsates inside me, his lips brushing my shoulder as he groans.

While he holds onto me, I feel more alive than I've ever felt.

CHAPTER 15

With the help of the guards, Elena brings me a bunch of boxes with clothes and shoes. I stare at the boxes in wonder.

"Ma'am, you need to pick something comfortable for going outside," Elena says, and my eyes widen even more. "A pair of pants and a sweater so you don't get cold. Something from these two boxes." She points at them. "I'll unpack the rest while you're away."

Away? I guess I'll be going for a walk again, but maybe it'll be a bit longer this time or farther away from the house so that Elena has enough time to sort through all the clothes and put them in the closet.

I grab a pair of dark blue jeans and a green sweater, and go to the bathroom. Once I'm dressed, Elena smiles at me and offers me a pair of black boots.

"Master is waiting for you outside," she says after I put on the boots.

I blink at her.

Dante?

I'll be taking a walk with him?

When I step out of the room, the guards observe me carefully, and I head down the hallway.

No one tries to stop me or asks me where I'm going. They just trail after me, but now there are only two of them while the rest stay behind.

I guess I'm not such a huge threat anymore.

When I exit the front door, my lips part in surprise.

Dante is leaning against the hood of a dark blue sports car, and as soon as he sees me, he straightens his back.

"Come," he says, opening the passenger door, a smile on his face.

"Where are we going?" I ask as I get in the car.

"Not far. You'll see."

I furrow my brow.

He closes the door and goes around the car so he can get in the driver's seat. Sitting so close to him is a little distracting, especially when he grins at me.

"My property is huge," he says. "We could walk, but I don't want to waste any precious time."

As he brings the engine to life, I can barely believe this is happening. Okay, maybe we're not going anywhere far away from here, but I haven't been away from the house for weeks now.

I want to see other things.

Something new.

Two cars join us on the road. Have to be the guards. I guess they don't want to take any risks when it comes to Dante's safety.

We pass through the thick trees and end up going past a huge field. A couple of minutes later, Dante pulls over in front of a one-story house.

We get out of the car, and an armed dark-haired man comes out of the house and greets Dante. While Dante is talking to the man, I look around.

It's kind of nice here.

Peaceful.

Birds are chirping. The sun is half-hidden behind a cloud.

It's not too cold or too warm either.

Just perfect.

"Caterina," Dante calls, and I turn my head to look at him.

He waves at me, and I follow him behind the house.

The first thing I see is a stable. When we go closer, I spot a black horse, and an excited gasp escapes my throat.

I love horses!

I rush toward the horse, but then I glance at Dante, unsure if we're here for something else.

I don't know who the man is and I don't want to get shot for doing something I'm not supposed to do. Dante just smiles at me, and I'm right in front of the horse a second later.

"Hey, beautiful," I say, running my hand down the horse's neck.

The horse neighs happily as I admire it.

"Looks like you made your choice," Dante says, and I furrow my brow until I see another horse.

It's dark brown, and I immediately go to it and caress its mane.

"You're beautiful too," I say, then turn to Dante. "Are they yours?"

He nods. "This one is Fire, and the black one's name is Spirit. Which one do you like more?"

"I don't know. I mean, they're both perfect."

"You can only ride one, so you'll have to choose."

My eyes bulge. "Ride? Really?"

"Yeah. Do you know how to—"

"I do." Riding is also one of those few things I managed to learn by pure luck. "I just need to refresh my memory. It's been a while."

One of my father's business partners had horses, and he insisted on my whole family visiting his ranch more than once.

Since the guy didn't know who and what exactly my father was, and his business was actually legal, we all had to pretend we were a normal family, so my father had to take both my mother and me with him.

And while my father was busy convincing the guy to make a deal with him, I got to play with the horses, and a nice riding instructor taught me everything she could.

I was super disappointed when the guy finally signed the deal and we no longer got to go.

"You should pick Spirit," Dante says. "He likes you, and he doesn't like many people."

"Yeah, sure." I flash him a smile.

Spirit and I were an instant match anyway.

"Which one do you usually ride?" I ask as he helps me get into the saddle, his strong arms pushing me up.

"Spirit."

My eyebrows arch.

He's letting me ride his favorite horse?

Why?

He gets on Fire's back, and then we head out toward the empty field that seems endless. I can barely see the trees in the distance.

"Race me," Dante says, and takes off.

I grip the reins, urging my horse to go faster. We rip through the field, and I catch Dante smiling at me when I get closer to him.

As I keep my eyes in front of me, I realize this might be my chance.

My chance to get away.

I haven't thought about it for a while, but now the opportunity is here.

But where do I go?

I don't know if there's a fence surrounding Dante's property. There has to be something to stop his enemies from getting too close. The guards have to be somewhere.

If I try something now, there will be no coming back, and if I fail, I'll pay dearly for it. I don't think Dante would just forgive me.

I meet his gaze.

There's something in his eyes. He's watching me carefully, as if he's waiting for me to try to escape.

And maybe it would work, but I don't think I should rush it. I'd have to see a map of this area first.

Otherwise, I'll just get lost and my horse will get tired. Or the guards will come after me in their cars, or I'll run straight into them.

I don't want something to happen to the horse either.

Forcing Spirit to go even faster, I glance at Dante, and when I see a wooden fence in front of us, I slow down.

"Do I win?" I ask.

He watches me for a few long moments as he stops next to me. "Yes, you do." His face is serious, but then a grin pops up on his lips. "But you won't win the second time!"

He takes off in the opposite direction, back the way we came from.

"Hey!" I let out an annoyed groan, and then I follow him.

As the air whips my face and I race after Dante, I strangely feel free, even though I know it's only an illusion.

CHAPTER 16

I watch Dante as he gets off his horse. My mind wants to make me feel guilty for enjoying riding with him because I ruined my chance to escape.

But maybe I didn't.

Maybe I just spared myself.

There was absolutely nothing indicating that I would've been able to be fast enough to get away.

Besides, I'm on Dante's horse, and he probably knows a few tricks to get him to stop, or maybe he's even trained him to do whatever he wants him to.

If not him, someone else would've probably stopped me.

I have to be more patient. I've already made a few rash decisions, and none of them have worked out so far.

The best thing I can do is wait.

For now.

If I'm going to escape, I have to be at least sixty percent sure that I can make it.

Yeah, all I have are maybes and guesses. But don't I deserve a few moments where I can just feel a little bit happy and enjoy the moment, without thinking about my situation?

Am I not allowed to find something good in all this?

Dante makes his way to me and helps me get off Spirit's back. When he catches me, I wind my arms around his neck so I don't fall.

Our gazes meet, and for a few seconds, it's like the time has stopped.

His mouth finds mine, and as he kisses me, he spins us around and carries me toward the stable.

When my back hits something, I let out a low groan, but Dante keeps kissing me, his hands already slipping under my sweater.

"Wait, what if someone—" I try to say when his lips move to my neck.

But damn, his mouth is igniting a fire inside me, and I can barely focus on my words when he grabs my breast through my bra.

"Doesn't it make the whole thing more exciting?" He briefly grins at me before pushing his lips against mine again.

His hand travels down my stomach and squeezes into my jeans, popping the button open. Warmth fills my insides, and I decide that yes, this is exciting, and yes, I want him.

He rubs my pussy through my wet panties, and I push toward his fingers, needing more. Somehow, he manages to yank my jeans and panties down and I step out of them. My sweater ends up on the ground next.

Dante tugs my bra down, exposing my breasts.

I let out a moan as he kneads my breast and twirls his finger around my nipple, and then his hand travels down, caressing my stomach.

All I know is that I want him inside me, as soon as possible. He pulls his shirt over his head and lets it fall to the ground.

After he toys with my breasts some more, his hand shifts to my cheek and he pulls me in for a demanding kiss that leaves me breathless.

I don't think I can take it anymore, so I brush my hand against his erection through his pants. He lets me unzip his pants, and I stroke his thick length through his underwear.

In one swift move, he pushes his pants and underwear down. I close my hand around his cock, my thumb circling his tip.

He groans, closing his hand over mine and making me move it faster.

I watch him as fire fills his eyes and his lips part as I keep rubbing him.

He pulls my hand away and tugs me with him. After he sits down on a big log, he pulls me to him.

I wonder if someone's watching us, and deep down, there's some part of me that's embarrassed, but when my gaze falls on Dante's hard cock, I know I don't want to keep my need in check right now.

I straddle him, holding onto him, as I lower myself down on his thickness. Closing my eyes for a moment, I groan as I stretch around him, taking him all in.

His hands roam up and down my back, and he smacks my ass as I start moving, impaling myself on him.

He kisses my shoulders and neck as our hips meet over and over again. I tightly wrap myself around him, enjoying the feeling of his strong, warm body against mine.

He thrusts into me, and my insides throb and tingle.

I throw my head back, trying to stifle a moan so that the whole world doesn't hear me. A choked sound comes out of my throat as I slam myself down on him.

His cock hits all the right spots deep inside me, and I cry out as my orgasm ripples through me, leaving me gasping for breath.

Dante holds me for a while longer, and then he lifts me up before getting us both to our feet.

"We don't want to leave any evidence lying around," he whispers, a wicked shine in his eyes.

I look at him for a few moments, unsure what he means. But then I see him stroking his cock.

I go down on my knees before he can say anything else and open my mouth wide. Excitement fills his eyes as he keeps stroking himself.

His cock brushes my lips, and then he comes into my mouth with a content sigh.

I keep my mouth open, my tongue circling his tip for a bit. When he pulls away, I close my mouth.

His hand lowers to my neck as I swallow, and he traces the movement of my throat with his finger.

I lift my gaze to his.

"Perfect," he says as he helps me get to my feet. "You're perfect."

Voices ring out from somewhere not too far away from us.

My eyes go wide, and Dante laughs. I scurry to get my clothes, trying to get dressed as fast as possible.

Amusement still dances in Dante's eyes as he lazily zips up his pants and picks up his shirt.

Once I'm dressed, I let out a sigh of relief. But when I look at Dante, I can't help but think that this was so much fun. No one has ever made me feel like this.

It was another moment of complete freedom and excitement.

If I manage to escape, I think I'm going to miss him.

It's a strange thought, but he's made me feel so many different things already, and I'm not sure if there'll ever be someone like him.

CHAPTER 17

When Elena brings me breakfast the next morning, I realize there's something different about it. She doesn't lock the door behind her.

I don't know if it's a mistake or if it's deliberate.

I pad over to the door and poke my head into the hallway. The guards are at the end of it, but there are fewer of them now.

Elena shows up again, her eyes meeting mine, and I almost duck back into the room as if I just got caught doing something I shouldn't.

"It's all right, ma'am," she says with a smile on her face. "Silly me, I forgot to tell you. Master said that you can go all over the house as you please."

I gape at her.

Wow, now that's a pleasant surprise. I immediately explore the house and find out that there's a small library, Dante's office that's locked, a living room with a TV, and a whole lot of other rooms.

Some are locked.

Some are empty.

But it's like a whole new world has been opened to me.

I wonder what changed Dante's mind. Have I finally gained his trust? Has he relaxed around me?

I don't want to think about it because I'm just so incredibly glad I don't have to be stuck in my room all the time.

Loud voices catch my attention, and I follow the sound. One of the voices belongs to Dante. I'd recognize it anywhere.

I don't know if I'm supposed to hear any of what he's saying, but my curiosity wins and I follow the sound. If Dante wants me to leave, I will.

But maybe he doesn't.

I reach another huge room that's almost identical to the living room. There are plenty of dark blue sofas around a few small tables, but there's no TV.

Dante is pacing up and down the room, and there's a man with dark brown hair and eyes who I've never seen before sitting on one of the sofas with a worried look on his face.

"How the fuck did this happen?" Dante yells, and then his gaze lands on me.

"Sorry," I say softly. "I didn't mean to interrupt. I can just—"

"No, it's fine," Dante says. "Sanders, this is my wife."

"Nice to meet you, ma'am," Sanders says with a small smile, and I return it.

"Okay, back to business." Dante snaps his fingers. "Tell me what happened. I want every single detail. Don't leave anything out, even if it doesn't seem important to you."

"Your uncle's men breached our territory, and Matteo went to confront them with a small group of men. It looked like an easy operation, but it was a trap, and your uncle has them."

Dante runs his hand over his face.

I don't think I've ever seen him so worried and distraught.

"Do you know where they are?" he asks.

"Yes," Sanders says.

Dante's head snaps to him. "Then what the fuck are you waiting for?"

"Sir, it's another trap." Sanders licks his lips. "The place where your uncle is holding everyone... It's very close to a police station, and even if we go around it somehow and try to keep things as quiet as possible, it's very likely your uncle already tipped them off something will go down, and they're just waiting for us to show up."

"The cops? Seriously? Does my uncle have no honor? How can he—" He clamps his mouth shut, his fingers clenching into fists. "Forget it. I don't give a fuck. It's me my uncle wants. Call him. He can have me."

"But sir!" Sanders jumps to his feet, his eyes bulging. "You can't do that!"

"It's my fucking decision." Dante bares his teeth. "I'm not going to let Matteo and the others die because of my mess!"

"We can find another way, sir," Sanders says. "Please be patient."

"All right. You have an hour. Figure something out. But don't expect me to just sit here and do nothing, because that's not going to happen." Dante's eyes flash with determination.

The kind of determination that can level a whole city.

I'm impressed. Who would've thought Dante would care so much about the people who work for him?

"I have a map," Sanders says. "Do you want to see it?"

"Yes!"

Sanders awkwardly pulls the map out of his pocket and almost trips as he tries to spread it over one of the tables.

Dante sits down on a sofa and leans forward, studying the map.

"The red circle is where—" Sanders starts to say.

"Yeah, I know," Dante snaps.

I inch closer and take a seat next to Dante. He doesn't seem to mind as I take a closer look at the map too.

"What about this street?" Dante points his finger at it. "Even if they're waiting for us, they can't be too obvious about it. They're not going to want to let everyone know what's up. It would be a disgrace on both sides. They'll want to make it look like they accidentally got alerted of our presence, and my uncle will pretend that he's surprised by the whole thing."

I can see the red circle where Matteo and the others are supposedly being held, and the blue circle that probably marks a police station.

"We won't be able to get away fast enough. They'll see us and block us before we can get out of this area." Sanders' finger moves over the map. "And we can't go through this part because we'd enter the Camayos' territory."

"Fuck," Dante mutters under his breath. "That son of a bitch. He's thought of everything."

"Unfortunately, it looks like it," Sanders says. "But if you could ask Matteo what he wanted you to do, I'm sure he'd say—"

"Don't." Dante shoots him a glare, and Sanders goes quiet. "Matteo would die for me. For any of us! Don't you think he deserves that we do everything in our power to save him? He's been my second for years, and he's proven over and over again that he's the best for the job. And most of all, he's a friend."

"I'm sorry, sir," Sanders says. "I didn't mean to disrespect—"

"Shut up. We don't have any time to waste." Dante's brow furrows as he stares at the map. "What about this alley behind this building? We can get to it unseen if we approach from the west." He traces his finger over the map. "This area over here is no one's territory. It's big enough that they can't have their eyes everywhere. Our scout can check for any cameras. And this alley is perfect."

Sanders tilts his head and pulls out his phone. "Please give me a moment."

He rapidly taps the screen, and I wonder if he's contacting the rest of Dante's men.

Dante brings his fist to his mouth and bites down on his finger.

A couple of minutes later, Sanders' phone beeps. He checks the screen and licks his lips.

I guess that's not good news.

"Romero says that it would be a good idea, but getting out of that alley will leave us vulnerable, and we'd be out there in everyone's sight for at least thirty seconds," Sanders says.

I'm a little lost because I have no idea who Romero is, but when I focus on the map, I realize getting out of the alley Dante wants to use would force them to go around another building before they can reach their target.

"Then what the fuck does he suggest?" Dante asks.

"We need more time to come up with a plan," Sanders says.

"And we don't fucking have it! What are we going to do? Drop down from the sky?"

I crease my brow. "Maybe you should."

Both Dante and Sanders look at me as if I just sprouted a second head.

"Caterina, I know you want to—" Dante starts to say.

"I don't mean literally drop out of the sky. How high are these buildings? Can you climb onto the roof and jump over? They shouldn't be able to see you or expect you there."

Dante's lips part, and I can almost see the wheels behind his eyes turning.

Sanders is still gaping at me like a fish.

"What are you waiting for?" Dante says to Sanders. "Check with Romero if my wife's idea would work."

"Yes, of course. Right away, sir." Sanders focuses on his phone.

Dante studies the map again. He reaches out to me, and his hand ends up resting on mine.

Sanders' phone beeps, and both Dante and I lift our heads, giving Sanders expectant looks.

"He says it might work, but it won't be easy. We need

to break into one of the buildings to get to the roof. The other roofs are very close to one another, so it's possible to jump over. We'll be right above our enemy's head. But we'll need a very good team who can do this stealthily enough."

"Yes, yes. Just tell him to gather all the details and send everything to me. I'll be on the team," Dante says.

Sanders opens his mouth.

"No. Discussion's over. You're dismissed."

Sanders dips his head and rushes out of the room.

"What would I do without you?" Dante shifts closer to me and presses his lips against mine. "Thank you."

I give him a small smile, glad that I could be of help.

Maybe I don't know the others who were captured, but I know Matteo. He doesn't seem like a bad guy.

But I don't know how I feel about Dante being part of the rescue mission. It's a very big risk for him, especially when he knows his uncle wants him.

But I also know there's no way to convince him to stay behind. If my friend were in danger, I would've done everything in my power to save them.

All I can do is hope that everything will turn out well.

CHAPTER 18

I HAVE TO FIGHT THE URGE TO BITE MY FINGERNAILS AS I wait for Dante to return or to hear any news about him and his mission.

Ever since he's left a few hours ago, my stomach has been doing nervous flips, and I don't know what to do to calm my nerves anymore.

I shouldn't be worrying so much.

Dante has probably done stuff like this a billion times. All this is just new to me, and I hate that I can't see what's going on.

Even though I have all kinds of distractions at my disposal now, even books, TV, and video games, I can't seem to focus on anything for more than five seconds. My thoughts just keep flying to Dante, and I want him to return home safely.

I keep telling myself it's because I don't know what

will happen to me if he dies. If he doesn't come back, will his uncle take me as his possession?

The thought of it makes me nauseated. I may not know anything about Dante's uncle, but since he doesn't even want to hear his nephew out before attacking and threatening everything he has, then I don't think he's a good man.

A good man?

My mind laughs back at me.

There are no good men in the mafia. Not completely good anyway.

But I refuse to believe things are always black and white. There's a whole lot of gray, and I don't know why Dante's uncle won't consider it.

I wouldn't be surprised if he knows how cruel Dante's father and brother were to him. There must've been some signs, even if they were lying about everything.

I close my eyes for a moment.

If Dante doesn't return, I'll have to run. But for some reason, I can't even think about it. Maybe he's ordered his men to kill me if that happens so his uncle won't get his hands on me.

I inwardly groan in frustration.

I don't want to consider any of those possibilities, and yet my brain is jumping to all kinds of crazy conclusions.

Leaning back on the sofa, I take a deep breath. It doesn't calm me much, but it clears my thoughts for a few seconds.

When I hear shouts, I spring to my feet and race toward the source of the noise, not even thinking that it might be dangerous for me.

The guards have gathered in the foyer, and when I get closer, they start clapping.

Dante steps through the front door, and my relief is so immense I almost collapse.

I dash toward him, not caring that the guards are staring at me, and some are even reaching for their weapons.

Dante's lips spread into a smile when he sees me, and I throw myself into his arms.

"You're alive!" I exclaim, and he lets out a grunt.

I immediately step away from him.

His jaw is tense, and he holds his arm over his chest. There's blood on his shirt.

"Oh, my god! You're hurt!" I bring my hand to my lips in surprise.

"It's nothing," he says. "I'll be fine."

"Are you sure? Do you have a doctor who can check up on you?" I try to lift his shirt to see the extent of his wounds, but he catches my hand before I can do it.

Right, we have an audience.

Everyone's staring at us.

"Yeah, I'm sure, and I don't need a doctor. Just a first aid kit from my room."

"I'll help you."

He nods, and I follow him as the guards start cheering again.

"I guess you saved Matteo and everyone?" I ask tentatively.

"Yeah. It wasn't easy, but your brilliant idea led us to a good plan, and we got them all out of my uncle's grasp."

"Where are the others?" I haven't seen Matteo or anyone else.

"They had to be taken to a doctor. My uncle had them tortured. But they're going to live." The way he says it makes it sound like it's something completely mundane that happens every day.

So normal to him.

But not to me.

I've never really seen all the dark and ugly that comes with being who we are.

"Oh. I hope they'll be fine," I say.

"It's here," Dante says as he stops in front of a door.

When he opens it, my eyebrows lift up.

His room is almost identical to mine. It's even mostly empty like mine. Sure, now I have a lot of clothes in my closet, and Dante's closet seems full too.

But there's nothing much in there.

I guess he has everything he needs in other rooms and just doesn't want any distractions while he sleeps.

But I'm a little surprised that he doesn't have any personal things or any photos. Okay, considering what went on with his father and brother, maybe he doesn't have any things or photos he wants to keep as memories.

But I thought he'd have some fun stuff or things that he likes. Something personal he doesn't want everyone to be able to see.

"What?" he asks, curiosity peeking out from his eyes. "What's that look on your face?"

"Nothing. I just thought your room would be more... I don't know."

"Bigger? Fancier? Darker? With human heads on the walls?" A smile quirks his lips, and I let out a laugh.

"Where's your first aid kit?"

"In the bathroom. I'll go get it."

"No." I get in his way, gently placing my palm against his chest. "You sit down and take off your shirt."

"Are you giving me orders now?" he teases.

"Yes. Yes, I am." I lift my chin up.

"Fine." He backs away from me with a smile.

I go to the bathroom and find the first aid kit in the cabinet. At least Dante has a mirror and cabinets in here, or I would've started to think he was his own prisoner.

I catch myself staring at my reflection in the mirror. I

look the same as always, I think. But I feel different somehow.

I blink and hurry to get to Dante.

When I see him shirtless, I nearly yelp and choke on my gasp.

There's a whole lot of blood and bruises on his chest.

"It's not that bad," he says when he sees the horror on my face. "Maybe just a few broken ribs and some superficial cuts."

"Just *a few* broken—" I shake my head. "Okay, I don't think most people would call this fine. Maybe you should—"

"Stop worrying about me. It'll heal. Just help me clean it up."

I sigh. "All right. But I would feel better if you saw your doctor."

There's something odd in the expression on his face, as if I just said something too crazy for him to believe.

After I open the first aid kit and grab what I need, I start cleaning up the blood, trying to be as gentle as possible.

Dante watches me, and I can see amusement in his eyes. He probably thinks I'm being too careful or something, which is insane because there's no way he's not in a whole lot of pain.

"Did you take any painkillers?" I ask.

"Don't need them."

When our gazes meet again, I wonder what would happen if I just stayed with him.

If I never ran away.

Maybe it wouldn't be so bad.

But who knows if any of this is real?

He might be using me.

Lulling me into a false sense of security.

Pretending to be someone he's not.

Maybe it's all just a funny game he's playing with me so he can eventually take pleasure in my pain.

Many have said he's a bloodthirsty killer, but is that really the truth? Being ruthless with his enemies doesn't seem all that terrible, especially when those enemies are willing to torture your friends to get to you.

I don't even want to think what Dante's uncle wants to do to him. If he really wants vengeance, I doubt he'll show any mercy or go for a quick kill.

No.

I know Dante.

I know who he is.

I know it better than anyone.

He's not a monster.

"What are you thinking?" he asks, and I jerk back.

"Nothing. Why don't you tell me how you did it?" I offer him a small smile. "I want to know all about your heroic mission."

"You do?" He narrows his eyes at me. "Are you sure?"

"Yeah, I want to hear everything. Even the gory details." I cock my head at him when his surprised look doesn't go away. "What? Do you think I can't handle it?"

"No, it's not that. I just didn't know if you'd care."

"Well, I do."

As he launches into his story, I refuse to think about anything other than this moment.

I focus on the here and now, and I enjoy listening to Dante's story as I take care of his wounds.

It looks like there are more and more of these moments that I actually want to treasure rather than forget, and that's something I didn't see coming.

CHAPTER 19

A LOT OF THINGS CHANGE AROUND THE HOUSE IN THE following days.

There are fewer guards around me, and I have a feeling they're with me for my safety rather than to keep an eye on me.

Dante and I spend more and more time together. We watch TV, have lunches together, and sometimes we talk about the books that we've read.

I'm even allowed to go into Dante's office.

It's not a very big room, and it has a desk with two chairs and a lot of shelves with books, files, and folders.

There is also a large cabinet full of weapons, but Dante keeps it locked most of the time.

I enter his office with a plate in my hand and put it on the desk. Dante looks up from his computer and furrows his brow.

"Where's Elena?" he asks. "You don't have to—"

"She's in the kitchen, and it took me a whole of convincing before she let me bring this sandwich to you. I just wanted to see you. I can carry a plate, you know." I give him a small smile.

"I know. I just thought... Never mind. Thanks." He focuses on his computer again.

"Can I know what you're doing? You've been in here for hours." And even though saying it out loud would be weird, I miss him.

I guess I got too used to having him with me all the time.

"I'm checking some of my accounts. I need to make sure that things add up."

"Don't you have an accountant for that?" I tilt my head.

"I do, but it's better when more people check what's going on, just in case there are any mistakes. And I want to make sure everything's okay."

"You can't be too careful, I guess." I shrug.

"Yeah." His forehead creases. "But I'm having some trouble figuring this shit out. The numbers I'm seeing here aren't what I expect them to be."

"Can I take a look?" I wonder if he'll let me see his accounts.

Maybe it's not something he's willing to trust me with.

His eyes lift to me, and he watches me for a few moments. "You wanted to get a degree in economics, right?"

I nod. "Yeah."

"Okay then. Help me figure this out." He gets up. "Sit."

I settle in his black leather chair and he leans on the headrest.

"This is what I'm seeing." He points to the right side of the screen and then to the left. "And that is what I'm supposed to be seeing."

I focus on the numbers and scroll through the files. "Um, yeah. Because it's not the same thing."

"How?" He groans.

"Well, it says at the top of the file that one of those includes taxes and the other doesn't." I crane my neck to look at him.

He runs his hand over his face. "And I spent an hour staring at it and trying to figure it out because I obviously can't read."

"Oh, come on. Don't be so hard on yourself. You've been working on it for hours. You're just tired. You need a break."

"Yeah, probably. Mystery solved. Thanks."

"Do you want me to check everything else that needs to be checked? I wouldn't mind."

"Yeah, sure."

After he shows me what he needs me to do, he takes a seat in the chair opposite from me, and as I work, he eats the sandwich I brought him.

My task isn't overly complicated, but it takes a lot of focus, which is a bit harder because Dante can't take his eyes off me.

"Done," I say when I finish. "Everything looks exactly as it should."

"Great."

A knock on the door startles us both, and I guess Dante isn't used to sitting in the other chair because he turns around too fast, making the chair scrape against the floor.

Maybe I distracted him enough that he didn't hear someone approaching the door, which made him feel disoriented for a bit.

"Come in," he says.

Matteo pokes his head inside. "Sir, I—" He goes quiet as he sees me in Dante's chair.

"I'm glad to see you're okay," I say to Matteo, who still has a few bruises on his face, but they're getting lighter every day.

He inclines his head to me. "Looks like I've been replaced," he says to Dante.

I get to my feet. They probably have business to

discuss and this small space will be overcrowded if I stay.

"What are you saying?" Dante asks.

"Nothing. Just that you won't need me as much anymore. You have your wife now. I'm happy for you, sir. I heard her idea helped you save my life. I hope you two will always be in love like this and look at each other like you do now."

Dante's whole body goes rigid.

Something's wrong, but I don't know what, even as I step closer to him. His face is blank.

"I think your pain medication is messing with your head and you're seeing things. But yes, I've always been good at managing my property, if that's what you mean," he says, his voice icy.

I stare at him, but he doesn't even look at me.

Property?

It's that what I am to him?

Even after everything?

I wait for him to tell me that I just misheard what he said or somehow misinterpreted it, but he's quiet, and even Matteo is gaping at him as if he can't understand what just happened either.

Tears prickle at the corners of my eyes, and I stride to the door.

Matteo gets out of my way, and when I burst into the hallway, he enters the office.

I take a shuddery breath, trying to stop myself from shaking.

I can't let this affect me so much.

Except, I can't stop my reaction either.

It hurts.

It fucking hurts.

I can't even explain how much. It's like my whole chest collapsed and cracked.

"There's no one outside to overhear us, so I'm just going to speak plainly," Matteo says. "What the fuck, man?"

"You may be my best friend, but I won't allow you to question me on this. This is none of your business. I played a game, and now I'm bored. That's all."

I don't wait to hear Matteo's reply.

I just break into a run and go straight to my room.

When I close the door behind me, I can't hold the tears back anymore. They fall freely down my face and I sink to the floor, hugging my knees to myself.

What I was afraid of has happened.

He tricked me.

He used me.

And like a fool, I believed him.

I fell for his act. It was all just a part of his plan to break me and humiliate me, and now he's gotten exactly what he wanted.

Just like always.

I'm so angry I want to scream, but I don't. Because if I do, someone will come to check on me, and I can't handle seeing anyone right now.

I should've tried to run away when I had the chance.

Now, I have no idea what will happen to me.

CHAPTER 20

I TOSS AND TURN IN BED BECAUSE I CAN'T STOP THINKING about Dante and about what he said. Getting some sleep seems impossible.

I keep asking myself how the hell I managed to be so stupid, because even though I had all the facts and knew what he might be doing, I pushed it all out of my mind.

Once again, I'm a victim of my own delusion.

Just like I believed my father would see reason, I believed Dante was different. I don't even know why.

I guess it was easier to live here and think that he... What?

Liked me?

Maybe even loved me?

I grab my pillow and put it over my head.

Dante hasn't come to see me after what happened at

all, and when Elena brought me food, she had a sad expression on her face for some reason.

I guess everyone has heard about what happened somehow. Matteo must've told someone, or maybe Dante did.

For all I know, he's drinking with the guys now and laughing about how he played his poor, little, dumb wife.

But the more I think about it, the more I believe I'm not actually crazy. I don't believe he's been playing me either.

Maybe I just want to believe something that isn't true to feel better about myself, but I don't think that's it.

What if Dante lied to Matteo?

But why would he do that?

I know him.

I'm pretty sure he hasn't been pretending with me, but why does he claim that's what's been going on?

I don't understand.

What did Matteo's comment trigger in him?

I yank my covers off me and get to my feet. If I don't go talk to him, I won't be able to stop thinking about it.

I need to know the truth.

I need him to tell me to my face that everything was a lie.

I quickly put on the first dress I grab from my closet,

and then I storm out into the hallway. Dante hasn't forbidden me from going out of my room again.

The guards watch me, but they don't say anything or move as I rush down the hallway. Once I get in front of Dante's room, the guards who are there watch me in confusion.

"Ma'am, you're not—" one of them tries to say, but I'm faster than them, and I grab the door handle.

Surprisingly, the door opens, and I burst into Dante's room. The lights automatically turn on.

He sits up in his bed, and judging by the dark circles around his eyes, he hasn't slept either.

Good.

"We need to talk." I glare at him.

The guards are at the door. "Sir, we didn't—"

"It's okay," Dante says, and they close the door. "Caterina, you can't just come here in the middle of the night."

"Why the fuck not? You owe me an explanation."

"An explanation?" His eyebrows shoot up, and that icy mask of his is back on his face.

No emotions.

Nothing.

Just fucking emptiness.

"Yeah. It's the least you owe me after everything," I say.

"There's nothing to talk about, and you shouldn't be

here. Actually, it's better if you leave before I lose my patience. If you disobey me, I'm not going to be merciful with you."

"What the fuck happened to you?" I narrow my eyes at him. "Do you want to make me think I'm losing my mind? Do you want me to believe that I imagined everything that happened between us?"

"And what happened between us, huh? You were useful to me. I fucked you and you liked it. Is that what you're referring to? Do you think it makes you special?"

I snort.

It's like I'm looking at a stranger.

Someone wearing Dante's face.

"This isn't you," I say. "I think you felt it too. The spark between us. You can't deny it."

He gets to his feet and stalks toward me. "I have no idea what you're talking about, but you need to get out of my room."

"Really? You're going to insist on that?"

"Are you going to keep annoying me?" He stops only inches away from me, and his hand closes around my throat. "You know what happens to things I no longer find useful."

Despite the pressure on my neck, I'm not afraid. I stare straight into his eyes, looking for the man I know he truly is, and not this...

Whatever this thing is.

"Did you forget who I am?" he says. "Do you really think I'd ever be capable of loving someone? You're living in a fantasy land. The sooner you realize that and wake up, the better for you."

"Fine," I spit out, grasping his hand and shoving it away from my neck. "You can keep living in your icy tower and not let anyone get too close. But when you freeze and die alone because you pushed everyone who cared about you away, don't be fucking surprised."

He steps away from me with a shocked look on his face, letting his hand drop to his side, and I spin on my heel and march to the door.

If this is how he wants things to be, then whatever.

I'll get out of this fucking place, and I'll get away from him.

He can go fuck himself.

I'm so angry I knock over one of the vases with flowers in the hallway on the way back to my room.

CHAPTER 21

Days go by, and I don't go out of my room so I don't have to see Dante. Just thinking about him makes me want to smash something.

And the worst part is that I miss him.

I miss talking to him.

I miss spending time with him.

And I miss his touch.

His lips against mine.

His arms around me.

A knock on the door makes me jump, but I remind myself it's just Elena. She's recently started knocking before she comes in.

I stare through the window and the bars, wondering how I can plot my escape, because if I stay here, I don't think I'll be able to survive.

Learning how to ignore Dante won't be easy, and I

don't even know what he plans to do with me. Maybe he'll just kill me so he doesn't have to deal with me.

"Caterina." Dante's voice makes me spin around. "I need you to check one of my accounts."

His voice is softer than usual, and there's a tiny crack in his perfect icy facade—his eyes. They're filled with an emotion I don't want to bother figuring out.

"Sorry, but I don't think I can help you," I say before I can stop myself, making my way to him. "I'm just a piece of your property, and I don't have a mind of my own. You should find a human being for that." I flash him a smile that I know doesn't reach my eyes.

He licks his lips. "I didn't... I didn't mean it like that."

"Then what did you mean?" I place my hand on my hip, raising an eyebrow at him.

"You're my wife."

I snort. "And your point is?"

He doesn't say anything, just watches me.

I scoff, turning away from him, but he catches my arm and pulls me to him. Our lips collide, and my mouth responds to his as he kisses me with all the passion in the world.

The fire inside me starts its usual dance.

I pull away from him and slap him so hard across the face that my palm stings.

His gaze doesn't leave mine, and I want to lock down the desire that I feel inside me, but maybe I shouldn't.

I want to feel good again.

I want to forget about everything else.

As if we're thinking exactly the same thing, Dante tips his head and I bring my lips to his.

Our kisses are full of fury.

Full of need.

Full of all the emotions neither of us really wants to talk about.

We tear at each other's clothes, and all I know is that I want to feel Dante's mouth on every inch of my skin.

When we're both naked, he picks me up and carries me to the bed. After he lowers me down and climbs on top of me, he kisses his way down my neck and takes my nipple into his mouth while his hands explore my body.

My breath leaves me in little gasps, and I bury my fingers into his hair. I grip the soft strands tightly, forcing his head down my body.

He looks up at me with a small smile on his face, and then I shove his head between my open legs. His nose rubs against my pussy, and I arch my hips.

His tongue dances across my opening, slipping in and out, and when he gently sucks on my clit, I feel like I'm going to burst from all the pleasure.

His tongue twists and swirls over my tender flesh, and soon I'm writhing on the bed as my release hits me.

"I need you inside me," I say when I catch my breath.

Dante looks up at me and lets me pull him up my body.

He positions himself between my legs, and his cock slides inside me, making us both groan.

I wrap myself tightly around him, trapping him between my thighs, my nails digging into the skin of his back as he thrusts into me.

My moans grow louder as he pumps into me, driving his hips into mine.

All I can think about is how he makes me feel, his body pressed against mine.

He moves inside me harder and faster, and I rake my nails down his back. He grunts, his punishing strokes bringing me closer and closer to the edge.

Our gazes meet as our bodies connect, and at that moment, we both cry out. My orgasm is so strong that all I can do is gasp for breath.

Dante collapses on top of me, his lips brushing my cheek.

Why does sex with him have to feel so good?

Why can his touch shatter me into pieces?

Why does he have to be such an asshole when it comes to us and our relationship?

I stare deep into his eyes, and I know the person looking back at me is my Dante.

The one whose fire can melt all the ice around his heart.

Why can't I just have him?

Always and forever?

After he rolls off me, I expect him to go back to his icy self, hop to his feet, get dressed, and leave, but instead, he snakes his arm around me and pulls me into his embrace.

I nestle in the crook of his arm and press myself close to him, wondering how long this nice moment will last as I trace my finger over his chest.

He kisses the top of my head and pulls the covers over us.

Warm, content, and safe.

That's how I feel.

CHAPTER 22

Once Dante leaves, I drift off to sleep.

When I wake up, I don't really expect anything because I don't want to get disappointed again.

Sure, we had a really nice moment yesterday, but I'm sure he'll find whatever excuse he's using to explain away what he's doing, and he'll be back to pretending he feels nothing.

A knock sounds on the door.

It has to be Elena with my breakfast. I sit up in bed because I'm actually starving.

The door opens.

But instead of Elena, Dante walks in with a tray of food.

I can see Elena behind him in the hallway, and I almost burst into laughter because the fear in her eyes as she watches him obviously means she's afraid he's going to spill something.

"Good morning," he says, placing the tray next to me.

Elena closes the door.

The glass with juice shakes a little, but it doesn't tip over.

I pick up a piece of toast and pop it into my mouth, almost moaning because it's so damn good.

Dante takes a seat on the edge of the bed, far away from me, and I know it's not just because he's afraid my juice will spill.

There's tension in his shoulders, and I feel like I'm about to lose him to Icy Dante again.

"Now what?" I ask. "Are you going to play hot and cold with me?"

"We're just having fun."

"It's more than that and you know it. Or do you bring breakfast to bed to every girl you fuck?" I cock my head at him.

He presses his lips into a tight line.

I guess the answer is no.

"You feel something for me, and I feel something for you. It's not just sex," I say. "I know talking about your feelings isn't something you're used to. I'm not used to it either. I mean, no one's ever talked about it in my family. I've never heard my father tell my mother that he loves her. It's just not something that ever comes up. And yeah, I'm confused too. It's all new to me too. But I don't want to pretend it doesn't exist or deny it."

"What does it matter what we feel? We are who we are. You said it yourself. It's not something people like us discuss or even consider."

"So what then? We're just puppets of the dark world we belong to? Can't we just be whoever we want to be?"

He stays quiet.

"Why don't we give ourselves a chance and see where this leads? Bottling everything up and putting on a brave face isn't going to make things better. It'll make them worse."

His eyes are swirling with emotion, but he still just looks at me as if he doesn't know what to say.

No, as if he's afraid that if he says something, he won't be able to take it back.

"I don't think you're a monster, or even a terrible person." My eyes bore into his. "Is that what's bothering you? Do you think I'm playing you? Do you think I'm just trying to make my life more comfortable? Do you think there's no way in hell I can feel something for you? Is that why you're pushing me away?"

"But I *am* a monster, Caterina," he says. "You just see what you want to see. You don't know all the things that I've done. You haven't seen me empty my gun into someone. You haven't seen me punch someone until their skull breaks. You haven't seen the blood on my hands."

"And how many of those people would've done the same to you if they had the chance, huh? How many would've shown you mercy?"

His jaw tenses.

The answer is zero, of course.

He doesn't have to tell me that.

"All I want is that you drop that icy charade you hide behind," I say. "I can't deal with two different people. I want you. Only you."

He looks away from me, and then his piercing gaze lifts to mine again. "Would you be saying any of this if you were free right now? If you had a choice, would you really want to have anything to do with me?"

I think about it for a few moments. "Actually, yeah. I would. We can't erase everything that happened. I got to know you better, and I know who you really are. I can't just ignore what I feel for you. I've never felt like this before, and I've never felt about someone the way I feel about you. I just know there's something between us, and I want to fully explore it. Why shouldn't we give ourselves a chance to be happy?"

"Don't you think you deserve better than me? Our lives are fucked up. You say that you've never felt like this before, and you've never gotten a chance to truly experience and enjoy your life. You think I make you happy. You think you have feelings for me. But it's only because you've only ever been with me. How can you be sure this is it? How can you be sure there isn't someone out there who would make you so much happier?"

I don't know what to say.

Maybe there is some truth in his words.

"You're right. I haven't really gotten a chance to date someone, but that doesn't make my feelings for you any less valid. Instead of meeting you at a bar, we met how we met. Do you think I wanted to have feelings for you? Do you think I didn't try to fight it? But we are where we are, and we are who we are. Why not give us a chance? If it doesn't work out, it won't work out. But at least we'll know."

He's quiet as I finish my breakfast.

When I move the tray onto the nightstand, I give him an expectant look.

"And? What did you decide?" I ask.

He shifts closer to me, his hand covering mine. "Okay."

It's just one small word, and he looks absolutely terrified to say it.

But he said it anyway.

"Okay?" I hold my breath, wondering if he's actually referring to something else.

"Yeah. We can give it a shot. If that's what you want."

"It is. But if you want it to work, you have to treat me like an actual human being. I'm not your property."

"I know. I'm sorry I said that. I just... I'm not used to being in a relationship."

"So that really means you've never been in a relationship before and you're not just in denial about what it was?"

He shakes his head. "I've never dated anyone either. It was all always just about sex. I didn't even ask for their names. The less I knew about them and the less they knew about me, the better."

I grimace. "I hope you got tested after all that."

"Of course. I always do."

"One more thing. If you want to be with me, then there can be no one else. If you're just going to leave me here and go find someone for sex, then we're not for each other. I don't like to share."

Maybe my mother and other women like her put up with it, even though they hate it, but I won't do it.

I can't.

If he's going to be mine, he's going to be only mine.

"Neither do I."

"Then we have an agreement. We're going to try the whole relationship thing and see where it leads us." A smile spreads across my lips.

"Sounds good." He leans toward me and brushes his lips against mine.

As he deepens the kiss, I wonder what will happen next for us.

Maybe this will work, or maybe it won't.

But I need to know.

I don't want to just walk away without finding out if Dante is truly the one for me.

A tiny voice in my head is telling me that my effort is futile.

Eventually, everyone betrays me. My father did it when he married me off despite my wishes. My mother did it when she refused to help me.

And Dante...

I wonder if he'll reject me too.

CHAPTER 23

IN THE FOLLOWING FEW WEEKS, DANTE AND I DO A LOT OF things together.

We go out on dates. He takes me riding. We're together most of the day, except when he has to deal with business, so if it's not something I can help with, I just go read a book.

Tonight, he's going to take me somewhere special. That's all I know, and it's all he was willing to tell me. All he asked was that I picked something elegant because the place where we're going requires it.

I take a look at my reflection in the mirror and apply some red lipstick to my lips.

I've moved into Dante's room, and he brings me everything I ask for. My makeup box is one of those things.

Even though I have to stay in this house, I'm not really his prisoner anymore, or at least I don't feel like it.

He even got me a credit card so I can order whatever I want online. I just can't have it delivered directly to our house. It has to go to one of Dante's secret houses, and after his men check that I'm not going to get a free bomb with the things I ordered, they bring everything to me.

I spin around in my long red dress.

I just like the color.

It's both sexy and not too revealing. Just the way I like it.

Satisfied with my look, I slip on my brand new red high heels and grab my small purse. When I'm done, I open the door.

Dante's in the hallway, lounging against the wall, his phone in his hand. His gaze lifts to me, and his lips part as he takes me in.

"Wow," he says, pushing himself off the wall and tucking his phone in the pocket of his black suit jacket.

"You look good too." I grin.

And really, his suit fits him just perfectly. He offers me his arm, and I take it. We head down the hallway.

When we pass the guards, I can feel some of them leering at me.

"Hey," Dante snaps at one of them. "What are you staring at?"

The guard mumbles an apology and focuses his gaze in front of him.

Dante takes me to his car and opens the door for me. I have to be careful of my dress as I get in.

"Can I know now where we're going? Maybe just a hint?" I bat my eyelashes at him when he gets in the car.

He leans toward me, and his lips graze mine. "No."

I pout, which makes him smile.

It's getting dark outside, but I can still see the guards following us in their cars once we're on the road.

As Dante keeps driving, I wonder if he owns some other nice place that I'm not aware of.

But after a while, more and more houses appear in view, and the city lights flash brightly in front of us.

I glance at Dante, my lips parting in surprise. "Are we going to the city?"

"Maybe."

I can barely believe it, but it's kind of nice to see other cars and people once we reach a more populated area. The city lights are getting closer and closer, and my excitement only grows.

I nearly plaster my face to the window as I watch the shops, bars, and people as we pass them by.

Dante pulls over in a parking lot, and while I'm still trying to figure out where we are and where exactly we're going, he gets out of the car and opens the door for me, offering his hand to me.

I let him help me to my feet. He spins me in the direction of a brightly lit restaurant. It's one of those expensive restaurants that everyone wants to go to—if they can afford it—and the wait-list is usually huge.

Dante takes my hand again, and we stroll to the entrance. I keep looking around because it's a bit weird to be among people again.

They don't know anything about me.

They don't know who I am.

I'm just another regular person to them.

It's refreshing.

Dante tugs on my hand, and I realize we're being led to our table already. It's a really nice table at the back of the restaurant. Separated from the rest.

Just for us.

There are candles and red roses everywhere.

Dante pulls out a chair for me and I take a seat.

"Do you like it?" he asks as he sits across from me.

"I love it!" I can't stop smiling.

Actually, my cheeks are starting to hurt, but I don't care.

I'm happy.

Dante's smiling too, and when we get the menus, I'm not sure what to choose.

"You can order all of it, and then choose what you like." He must've seen me frown at the menu a little too hard.

"No, I think I can narrow it down to two or three choices instead." I grin.

"Good."

As we wait for our food, we talk about a little bit of everything, and the time passes so fast I don't even notice.

When our food is on the table, everything smells so delicious that I'm not sure what to taste first.

"Try this." Dante lifts his fork with some pasta and sauce, and I open my mouth.

I keep my eyes on his as my lips close around the fork. Dante watches me with a spark in his eyes.

"Mmm. It's good," I say with my mouth full, and he laughs. "But you gotta try this."

I get a meatball on my fork and extended my arm to him. The meatball almost falls off the fork, but he closes his mouth around it fast enough.

I let a laugh. "Good?"

He nods as he chews.

We keep sharing our food, and when we get dessert, I play with my fork, licking chocolate off it while Dante carefully watches me.

"If you keep doing that, we'll have to find a little more private place," he finally says, his voice husky.

"Sure." I'd like that very much. "But first, I need a moment."

I get to my feet and head to the bathroom. Two men rise from their tables too.

The guards just won't let me out of their sight, will they? I'm pretty sure there's one of them in the kitchen too, to make sure nothing weird happens to our food.

For a second, I wonder if they're going to follow me in the bathroom, but they stop in the hallway, pretending they're discussing something.

I slip into the bathroom and smile at my reflection in the mirror. If someone had told me I'd be this happy, I wouldn't have believed them.

I fix my makeup a little. Since no one else is in the bathroom, I do a little dance to the music that's blasting in here. It's a quick, catchy song.

When I open the door, I stop dead in my tracks.

The guards are on the floor, unconscious.

"Hello, gorgeous," a dark-haired man says as he jumps out at me from behind the wall.

I open my mouth to scream, but he places something over my mouth and nose as he grabs me. I try to thrash against him, but it's impossible to fight him.

My head starts to swim, and black spots fill my vision.

Dante...

It's the last thing I think before I fall into the darkness.

CHAPTER 24

MY HEAD HURTS, AND I GROAN AS I TRY TO MOVE, BUT I can't.

Something's holding me down.

Or up.

I'm not sure, so I pry my heavy eyelids open.

As I blink at the dim room, my heart jumps into my throat. My wrists and ankles are tied to the chair I'm sitting in.

There are unfamiliar armed men everywhere around me.

Kidnapped.

Someone has kidnapped me.

Where's Dante?

I don't see him here.

Have they only taken me or do they have him too?

Panic grips my insides. If they have him, we're both going to die, aren't we?

And if not, then what do they want from me? What are they going to do to me? I can barely think as thoughts assault my brain, and I'm at risk of hyperventilating.

This wasn't supposed to happen.

Dante's men are always so careful with everything, and that one time we go somewhere fun, something bad happens.

I don't know how.

"You're awake," a man in a black suit says, as he steps in front of me.

His gray eyes stare at me as if he's trying to see into my mind. His dark brown hair is streaked with gray.

"Who are you? What do you want?" I ask.

If I talk to him, maybe I'll find out something. Maybe Dante hasn't been captured, and he's looking for me everywhere.

But will he find me in time?

"Relax, sweetheart," the man says. "You're only bait for now."

Bait?

A tiny sliver of hope sparks in my chest. Does that mean they don't have Dante? No one else would come for me.

Certainly not my father. I'm not his problem anymore since I'm married to Dante.

I don't have anyone else.

"He'll come for you." The man grips my chin, forcing me to look up at him. "Rumors are he's smitten with you. They say he might even trade his life for yours. I'm really curious to see where the truth lies."

"Who are you?" I ask once again, even though I fear I know the answer.

"Francesco Antonelli." His lips spread into a cruel smile. "Your husband's uncle."

Aw fuck.

It's exactly as I feared.

"What do you want with Dante?"

"Do you love your husband?" Francesco steps back and watches me as if I were an exotic animal in a zoo.

"Why do you care?"

"Because you're going to lose him."

I bare my teeth at him. I'd prefer if *he* lost his head instead.

Francesco turns to one of his men who's just stepped through the door. "Anything?"

"Not yet, but we sent the message," the man says.

"Good. If he doesn't respond in three hours, take her to the room."

There's something ominous about the way he says

the word *room*, as if it's some special room, different from others.

Do I even want to know what he intends to do with me?

"You are pretty." Francesco's fingers brush my cheek, and I turn my head away. "But nothing too special. Your pussy must be something then. If your husband doesn't return my call, I'll have some free time to check." His grin sickens me even more than his words.

Oh shit.

My throat constricts, and my every muscle is tight with fear.

I've never been this afraid.

"Why do you want to kill my husband?" I ask.

If he keeps talking to me, then maybe he won't get any insane ideas like the one he just mentioned.

"It's a family issue, you could say. I don't know if he told you, but your husband killed my brother and my nephew."

"So you're going to kill him to make it right? How does that even make sense? He's your family too." I don't really think this guy gets it, though.

He's clearly mentally unstable.

"He stopped being my family when he killed my brother." Francesco's face contorts with anger. "My brother was everything to me, and your husband killed him just to get something that doesn't belong to him.

Instead of finding a way to prove himself, he turned against his family."

"Do you even know what your brother did to Dante? He abused him! Anyone would've snapped and wanted to get free."

There's no surprise on Francesco's face.

"Abuse?" He laughs. "The boy was weak. All his father tried to do was make him powerful, and look at him now. It worked. Dante should've thanked him instead of killing him."

I blink at him.

Okay, now that's some seriously fucked up and twisted logic.

Or, better said, there's no logic at all.

He's rambling.

Why is anyone even working for him? Ah yes, he probably pays them well, so why should they care as long as they get paid?

"I found them." Francesco's eyes grow distant. "I found them in a big pool of blood. So many bullets wasted. I barely even recognized them."

I want to suggest that he should seek psychological help because he clearly has a whole lot of issues, and finding his dead brother and nephew only made those issues worse.

But if I say anything, he could snap and hurt me.

Come on, Dante.

Find me.

Please.

But what if he gives himself over to his uncle instead?

I refuse to think about it. He's not that stupid. He knows his uncle will kill us both or set up a trap for him if he tries to negotiate.

I have a feeling the only reason Dante hasn't killed his uncle too already is that, aside from being slippery, the guy is probably his only family left.

And since Dante has already had to kill two of his family members, he's probably been trying to avoid killing another. It would only add to his torment, because even though he feels relief they can't hurt him anymore, I'm sure things aren't that simple.

If someone told me my father was dead, a part of me would be glad, but another would be sad.

Sad for all the things we could've had and done if only there had been a way for him to see me as his daughter and not a pawn.

But some things will never happen, no matter how much we hope for them.

"Sir!" someone yells, and everyone in the room is instantly on alert.

"What?" Francesco barks. "I'm busy!"

"We are under—" He doesn't get to finish because the whole building shakes from what seems to be an explosion.

The men race out of the room with their weapons drawn as gunshots echo everywhere.

Francesco looks at me. "So he does care about you."

He says it as if it's the weirdest thing ever.

"And I thought he was strong. Looks like I was wrong." He pulls out his gun and points it at me.

My heartbeat pounds loudly in my head, and I thrash so much my chair tips over. I fall to the ground, trying to free myself and get away from Francesco before it's too late.

Annoyance flashes through his eyes as he tries to take aim at my head.

I'm too slow, and I can barely move.

I won't get out of this alive.

His gun is aimed straight at me, and I close my eyes.

Shots ring out through the room, and my whole body trembles.

But I don't feel any pain.

Nothing.

"Caterina!" Dante's voice pierces the air, and my eyes fly wide open.

He goes down on his knees next to me, a panicked look on his face, his eyes bulging and full of emotion. His arms wrap around me as he removes the rope from my wrists and ankles.

"Fuck," he whispers as he plants multiple kisses on

my head. "Are you okay?" His worried gaze travels my body.

"Yeah." I glance to my right.

Francesco's body lies on the floor. His head is a mess of blood, which is pooling under him.

Dante must've emptied his gun into him.

He follows my gaze and flinches.

I look at him.

"If you don't want me to touch you—" he starts to say.

I press my lips to his, and he kisses me back.

"I'm glad you killed that monster. He was insane," I say softly. "I know he was your uncle, but—"

"Yeah, I know. I kept hoping for a miracle. He was my only family left and I just..."

"You have me now." I offer him a small smile.

He pulls me into his arms again.

"How did you find me so fast? I thought he would do terrible things to me." I pull away a little so I can look into his eyes.

"There's a tracker in the heel of your shoe. My uncle's men didn't figure it out."

"Oh." Now that sounds like something useful, but if I'd been trying to escape him, I would've had a problem.

"I would've told you about it, but Matteo forgot to tell me when he brought the shoes," he says. "He only told me after you were gone. I thought you were dead."

His eyes are glassy. "If anything had happened to you, I would've never forgiven myself. I can't believe my uncle managed to sneak his men into that restaurant."

"It's not your fault." I place my hand on his arm.

The gunfire ceases, and when someone runs into the room, Dante immediately shields me with his body.

"Are you okay?" Matteo asks.

"Yeah." Dante's shoulders relax. "We are."

And that's the only thing that matters.

AFTER I TAKE A LONG SHOWER, I GET DRESSED. DANTE IS pacing up and down in our room, a frown creasing his brow.

"Is everything okay?" I ask.

"Yeah." He straightens his shoulders and approaches me, so we're only inches apart. "I have something for you."

"What is it?"

He pulls a small black box out of his pocket and hands it to me.

I stare at the box in surprise.

"A gift," he says. "For you."

I open the box.

There's a key inside.

"I don't understand," I say.

It doesn't look like a car key. Just a regular key.

"It's the key to your apartment." His lips spread into a forced smile.

"Okay, now you completely lost me. Why do I need an apartment?"

"So you can go to college again."

My jaw hits the floor. "What?"

"It's what you want most, isn't it? To get your degree? Now you can. You're free."

"Whoa, slow down. I *do* want to go to college. But what about us?"

He shrugs. "You were forced to marry me and be with me. I'm giving you your freedom back. You'll have everything you need and my protection. We just can't officially divorce."

"Are you breaking up with me?" My eyes fill with tears.

This has to be the happiest and the saddest day of my life.

"Yes." He licks his lips.

"But—"

"I've made up my mind, Caterina. I want you to be happy. I want your dreams to come true, and they won't if you stay here with me."

"That's bullshit!"

"I'm sorry. But it's for the best." He presses his lips to my forehead, and then he goes to the door.

"Dante," I call after him, but he just leaves.

I stare at the key.

And then my heart breaks into pieces.

I gained something.

A new chance at life.

But I lost something too.

My chance at love.

And I don't know if I'll ever get it again.

CHAPTER 25

It takes me a few months to stop feeling like a zombie who's walking around on autopilot.

I still miss Dante so much that I can't even explain it, and I always bury myself in work so I don't have to think about him.

Sometimes it works.

Sometimes it doesn't.

Many times, I think about contacting him, but I don't.

He doesn't want me in his life.

No one ever does.

They just get rid of me and move on.

I'll have to find happiness on my own, even though I don't know how.

The more time passes, the more I'm sure what I feel for Dante is real love.

The thing I've always secretly dreamed of and wanted whenever I read about it in books.

It's real.

It exists.

And it provokes so many feelings inside me that it's impossible to ignore.

When the day of my graduation ceremony comes, I stare at my reflection in the mirror. I want to be happy because I got exactly what I wanted.

I made it.

This is my day.

I proved to myself and everyone that I could do it. That I could be more than just my family's pawn.

Except, no one's here to share my joy.

My friends will have their families with them, and I'll have no one. I have no idea if my parents know anything about my achievement, but I doubt they'd care even if they found out.

More likely, they'd be pissed off. I'm being a terrible wife right now in their eyes.

I take a deep breath and steel myself. If I could finish college, then I can survive the ceremony.

After that, I'll just focus my energy on finding a job.

ONCE THE CEREMONY IS OVER, EVERYONE RUSHES TO THEIR families. There are hugs, photos, flowers, squeals…

I just smile at everyone as I pass them by and try to get as far away from them as possible so they don't see I'm on my own. I don't want to ruin my friends' moments and have them worry about me.

But after I push through the crowd, I see three familiar faces. I blink, wondering if I'm hallucinating.

Except, I'm not.

Dante.

He's grinning at me, a huge bouquet of flowers in his hand.

Matteo is next to him.

Elena smiles at me, a box in her hands.

I run to them, tears filling the corners of my eyes. Dante catches me into his arms and spins me around.

"Congratulations," he says.

"We're so proud of you," Elena says when Dante lowers me to my feet. "I made some cookies for you."

"Thanks," I say.

"Why don't we take some photos?" Matteo suggests, and when he pulls out his phone, he snaps some photos of me and some of all of us together.

I press myself close to Dante, and memories flood me at the contact.

"We have more surprises for you," Dante says. "Come on."

The four of us end up going to a restaurant not too far away from my campus. We're the only guests, and I guess Dante doesn't want to take any risks this time.

There's a small dance floor in the middle, and as the music starts to play, Dante extends his hand to me.

"Wanna dance before our food is ready?" he asks.

"Yeah." I take his hand and let him pull me to the dance floor.

I wrap my arms around his neck, and as we stare into each other's eyes, his arms around me, it's like nothing has changed between us.

It's like we're back right where we're supposed to be.

But I don't know if that's true.

I don't know if he's here as my friend who just wants to make me happy, or if there's something more.

I have no idea what he's been doing.

Maybe he's dating someone.

"I missed you," he says.

"Did you?" I cock my head at him.

He nods. "There's something I want to tell you."

I give him an expectant look.

"I love you," he says, and I stop moving as I stare at him.

"What?" It's the stupidest thing I can say, but it flies out of my mouth anyway.

"Being without you... It's just made me realize that you were right. I have feelings for you. Strong feelings. I love you." The way he says the word *love* is a bit funny, as if he's not sure he's pronouncing it right. "I know it's a little too late. You probably want to move on with your life, and that's okay."

"No. That's not what I want. Dante, I love you too. I never stopped loving you."

A smile stretches across his lips, and then his mouth crashes against mine.

Every second we missed.

Every moment we were apart.

All of it comes together, and I can't stop kissing him.

"Will you be my wife? Again?" He presses his forehead against mine as we both try to catch our breaths.

"Yeah. Yes!" I let out a laugh.

"Do you want another wedding?" he asks. "A proper one, this time."

"Good god, no. Not my thing." One was more than enough for me.

It doesn't matter how it all started.

What matters is how we feel about each other now.

"I don't give a shit about ceremonies, or papers, or deals, or anything," I say. "I just want to be with you."

"Even if you know who I am and what I do?"

I nod. "But if you'd like to have a real wedding, I can—"

"No. We're already married anyway. But does this mean you're also willing to consider working for me?" He grins. "I have an open position for someone who knows how to handle my accounts and some other stuff."

"Um, yeah. I'll consider it. But the offer better be good." I wink at him.

"I have something else for you," he says. "It's outside."

I furrow my brow and let him lead me to the window. There's a red sports car in the parking lot with a huge bow on it.

"What?" My head snaps to him. "You got me a car? But I don't even know how to drive!"

"I'll teach you." He winds his arms around me from behind and nips on my earlobe.

It's so incredibly easy for him to ignite a fire inside me that it's almost like we were never apart.

"Can you say that thing to me again?" I crane my neck.

"What thing?"

"That three-word thing."

"I love you?"

I flash him a smile. "Yeah, that's the thing. See? You're getting better at saying it already."

"I love you, Caterina," he whispers into my ear, and I lean into him.

Now this is the happiest day of my life.

I've got everything I could've possibly dreamed of.

And even more.

"Your food will get cold!" Elena shouts from the other end of the room.

"Then we better hurry," I say. "And later, maybe you could, um, discreetly follow me to the bathroom? Just pretend you have to make a phone call or something."

Dante winks at me and takes my hand, and we stroll to the table.

When Matteo and Elena see us, they both smile.

"Finally," Matteo says, looking at me. "You won't believe how much he's been whining to me about you. I barely got him to leave the house. Nothing made him happy. Nothing. Couldn't even get a smile out of him."

"Fuck you!" Dante says, but he's smiling. "I didn't do any of that."

"Yes, you did," Matteo teases. "I have witnesses who can confirm."

As we take a seat at the table, I realize that I do have a family.

A family who isn't going to leave me or use me just to get what they want.

I glance at Dante.

My heart is whole again, and his is no longer made of ice.

AFTER I SLIP AWAY TO THE LADIES' ROOM, I CAN BARELY contain my excitement, and I can't stop grinning either.

Just knowing that Dante and I are sneaking around right now makes the whole thing even more thrilling. I just hope he'll manage to get away from Matteo and Elena.

When the door opens, I glance over my shoulder.

Dante approaches me with desire and hunger in his eyes. His arms tightly wrap around me from behind, and I lean on the sink counter, tilting my head as he lowers his lips to my neck.

I'm already burning with need as he tugs the strap of my dress down and kisses my shoulder as he keeps his gaze on mine in the mirror.

His hands roughly roam my body, and I can feel his erection poking at my back. The top of my dress ends up just below my breasts, and he yanks my bra down with so much force that the clasp snaps open.

He cups my breasts as his mouth closes around my earlobe, and I lean into him, my pussy already dripping and ready for him.

I missed him so damn much.

After giving my breasts a squeeze, his hands travel down my body and pull my dress up. He squeezes my ass and then gives me a few quick smacks that only increase the ache and longing inside me.

He pushes my panties down to my knees, and when his finger slips into my slickness, I let out a groan. He shoves another finger inside me and pumps in and out of me, making it hard for me to keep my moans down.

I still let out a small cry as he rubs my clit, spreading pleasure all over me. When his fingers pull away, our eyes meet in the mirror.

Dante slides the fingers that were inside me into his mouth and closes his eyes for a moment. "I missed your taste."

"I need you inside me." I push my hips back, rubbing myself against him.

"Beg for it," he says. "Tell me what you want."

"Please. I want your cock. I want you to fuck me."

A smile spreads across his lips, and I hear him unzip his pants.

He grips my hips, his cock grazing my entrance.

"Please!" My voice is full of urgency.

He plunges into me, slamming himself so deep inside me that I let out a gasp, and he sighs.

"I missed your tight pussy too," he says as he pounds into me, his thrust hard and fast.

I press my lips together, but my moans and groans

still seem too loud. My whole body is vibrating with intense sensations of pleasure as he rams his cock into me.

"Look at me," Dante commands as his hand wraps around my neck, and I find his eyes in the mirror. "Don't look away."

I obey as he thrusts into me, the pressure on my throat increasing.

My orgasm erupts through me as I stare straight into Dante's eyes. His hand clamps over my mouth and muffles a loud moan that escapes my throat.

He presses his mouth against my shoulder as his release rocks his body.

When he lets go of me, I have to support myself on the sink so I can catch my breath.

"We should do this more often," he says as he zips up his pants.

"Definitely." I flash him a smile as I pull my bra up.

My face is flushed.

My hair is a mess.

Dante's shirt is wrinkled.

There's no way in hell we'll be able to fool anyone about what we did.

But I realize I don't care.

EPILOGUE

"I have something for you," Dante says, and offers me a black box that he was hiding behind his back.

It's been five years since we got back together.

Five years of pure bliss.

Our room is now full of our photos, mementos, and all the things that make us happy.

Okay, there were a few issues here and there, but we overcame them all.

"What is it?" I eye him for a moment before opening the box.

It's a necklace.

A breathtaking diamond necklace.

A gasp escapes my throat.

"It's beautiful!"

"I'm glad you like it. It's for our get-back-together anniversary." He grins.

"Yeah, I know it's today." I grin. "Thank you. I love it! Can you help me put it on?"

"Of course." He takes the necklace, and I turn around so he can place it around my neck.

His fingers linger on my skin. "I have another gift for you. For us, actually."

I turn around to face him.

"You've been working very hard, and you're the main reason why our business is thriving so much."

"And you're the reason why all our enemies fear us." I grin.

No one has dared to challenge Dante's reign, and his territory keeps expanding, which makes us pretty much as safe as we can be.

He also found a loophole to get out of the deal with my father.

"We're going on a well-deserved vacation," he says. "I want to show you the whole world, and Matteo and I figured out how we can do it safely."

"Oh, my god!" I throw myself at him because I'm so damn excited I want to kiss him over and over again.

His lips find mine, and I melt into our kiss.

When we pull apart, my eyes bore into his.

"I love you," he says, making me smile.

"I love you too."

We used to be afraid of love, but now we're not.

I know we're going to be happy forever.

I can feel it.

###

ABOUT THE AUTHOR

Evelyn Ferras is the author of *I Despise You*, *Property*, and *Pretty Plaything*. She's loved reading romance ever since she was a teen, and her passion for strong heroines and sexy heroes only grows stronger every day.

Evelyn lives at the coast with her family and enjoys watching sunsets. Very often, she'll catch a sunrise too, especially when she's curled up with a book, binge-watching Netflix, or playing out stories in her head before writing them down.

Find her at evelynferras.com

www.ingramcontent.com/pod-product-compliance
Lightning Source LLC
Chambersburg PA
CBHW031125130726
47988CB00006B/2236